He'd never been kissed like this before, and he held her there, enjoying the journey through this uncharted and gentle place

She caressed the back of his head, and when he thought she was separating from him, he was filled with irrational longing, and he grabbed her arms and used his lips to capture her by the chin.

He'd seen animals mate on nature shows, their foreplay of nipping one another playful and gentle, and he understood that visceral animalistic instinct to claim one and make that one his own.

Purring started deep in her belly, and he put his arms around her, knowing she felt that magnetism too, and when the moans were nearly out of her, he sealed her mouth with his so they released into him.

The pressure of her mouth lessened and she eased off her toes, her hands busy at his waist. Her fingers tangled with his as they battled for who'd get his belt loosened first.

"Let me."

"I can do it faster," he tol

CARMEN GREEN

was born in Buffalo, New York, and had plans to study law before becoming a published author. While raising her three children, she wrote her first book on legal pads and transcribed it onto a computer on weekends before selling it in 1993. Since that time she has sold more than thirty novels and novellas, and is proud that one of her books was made into a 2001 TV movie, *Commitments,* in which she had a cameo role.

In addition to writing full-time, Carmen is now a mom of four, and lives in the Southeast. You can contact Carmen at www.carmengreen.blogspot.com or carmengreen1201@yahoo.com.

CARMEN GREEN

Sensual Winds

KIMANI
ROMANCE

To Lori Bryant Woolridge, Nina Foxx, Martrice Denson.
I'll cherish our friendship always.

To the Sparrow. I'll see you in the Rapture someday.

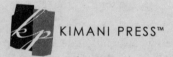

KIMANI PRESS™

ISBN-13: 978-0-373-86121-7

Recycling programs
for this product may
not exist in your area.

SENSUAL WINDS

Copyright © 2009 by Carmen Green

All rights reserved. The reproduction, transmission or utilization
of this work in whole or in part in any form by any electronic, mechanical
or other means, now known or hereafter invented, including xerography,
photocopying and recording, or in any information storage or retrieval
system, is forbidden without written permission. For permission please
contact Kimani Press, Editorial Office, 233 Broadway, New York, NY
10279 U.S.A.

This is a work of fiction. Names, characters, places and incidents are
either the product of the author's imagination or are used fictitiously,
and any resemblance to actual persons, living or dead, business establishments,
events or locales is entirely coincidental.

® and TM are trademarks. Trademarks indicated with ® are registered in
the United States Patent and Trademark Office, the Canadian Trade Marks
Office and/or other countries.

www.kimanipress.com

Printed in U.S.A.

Dear Reader,

To the sensual backdrop of Herbie Hancock's CD *Possibilities,* Brenda Jackson and I brainstormed our MOTHER NATURE MATCHMAKER novels over the phone one evening.

I am always honored to work with a master, and Brenda is one of the best in our profession. She's chock-full of ideas and always respectful of mine. Ironically, when we got on the phone, we both had our TVs tuned to the same station and the documentary was chronicling how Herbie created his masterpiece. My favorite song on the CD? "A Song for You."

I'm honored to have worked with Brenda and Celeste Norfleet on this series, and I want you all to enjoy our highly favored men of Key West. My thanks to Brenda and Celeste and to you all for giving us the opportunity to entertain you once again.

I'd love to hear your thoughts on my book *Sensual Winds.* Write to me at carmengreen.blogspot.com or carmengreen1201@yahoo.com.

Blessings,

Carmen

Chapter 1

There was a rhythm to New York City at 7:00 p.m. that no other city could duplicate. Throngs of people streamed down sidewalks and into streets, the innocuous traffic lights controlling every man and woman, car, taxi and bus.

Today Manhattan was a little different; brightened by the mayor, who'd declared it Smile Day. Dozens of volunteers had been dispatched around Manhattan to take pictures of anyone who was smiling, and then they were given their photo.

Today, everybody was smiling in New York City at dusk.

Ten floors up from the bustling streets, Doreen Gamble sat at her desk and touched the corner of her smiling photo. Her pace had been frenetic at lunch. She had been trying to balance a tray of two large cups of green tea, a boxy Crate and Barrel wedding gift for a coworker, a prized bag of Christian Louboutin silk lace-up sandals and a political magazine when she'd been asked if she wanted to brighten up New York with her smile. It didn't hurt that the photographers had goofy Smile tiaras on their heads.

They'd been so irresistible, she'd been glad to show off her whitened, otherwise uncorrected thirty-twos. She didn't even mind donating to the charity that supported the 9/11 memorial fund. She'd arrived back at work feeling as if she'd done some good for the world.

The back line rang, and her thoughts returned to the here and now. Doreen hoped it was Lucas. Lately, his no-news updates had left her disappointed, but she hoped he had some good news today.

"Good morning—*evening,* sorry," Doreen corrected, shoving her long hair behind her ear. "How may I help you?"

"You work so much you don't even know if it's day or night? Tell that woman of mine to give you a day off."

Lucas McCoy's voice had the power to make her feel as if even on her worst day she was the prettiest girl in the room. If he made every woman feel this way, it was no wonder he did more renovation jobs for women than men.

Who could help having a tiny crush on him? She couldn't.

"Put me on webcam, Doreen," he said. She blushed, wishing she'd had a few extra minutes to fix herself up.

Lucas wasn't her man, but she still didn't want to look bad to him.

She did as he instructed. "We're on. Hey there," she said, seeing the handsome man who was in his jeans and T-shirt.

"Hi." He waved. "Now, about the crazy hours you work. You need to stand up for yourself. Stomp around your desk with your picket sign. She'll get the hint."

Doreen laughed. "Yeah, okay. I like having a job. Besides, would she care? I don't think so. My job is to be here, at seven at night, waiting for a phone call from that crazy, distant place called Key West, and a man named Lucas who's calling to tell me about an Alfiere Italian sink. Tell me you have good news."

She'd said it all as if she were in a poetry reading, letting the words drop and roll in all the right places.

"I'm sorry." He shook his head, trying to look sad. "This is a 'bad news, good news' webcam call."

Doreen groaned. "I have to say, Lucas, I'm disappointed."

"And if you make that sound again, I'll be coming through the camera to make that disappointment go away."

"Lucas McCoy, you're an engaged man," she chastised, her neck burning at the volley. Lucas's good looks hadn't been lost on Doreen. She had always been attracted to tall men, considering she was five-ten.

He looked like the corporate type, too, with short hair and a sexy goatee, and smooth, chocolate-colored skin that reminded her of melted kisses. She knew from her boss that he was thirty; in fact, Emma had boasted about dating a man nine years younger. But Lucas was the perfect age for her, only a year older.

"Doreen, where has that wandering mind taken you?"

She shook herself. "Nowhere, Lucas. What did you say?" Guiltily she paid attention.

"You know my fiancée hasn't been down here in eight months, and if she doesn't get her butt down here soon, there'll be hell to pay."

"Emma wants to see you, but her promotion means big things here at Regents Cable." Doreen sat back in her chair and crossed her legs, relieved he still sounded playful. "She's the first black woman to hold the title of VP of urban development, and they're expecting great things from her."

"I know." Lucas didn't look like he cared one thing about the excuse. "I'm not begrudging her career success. Not for a second. But a man needs his woman, especially one he's proposed to. Anyway, we'll work it out. Meanwhile, let me update you on the renovations."

Happy to be on safer ground, Doreen rested her elbow on the desk and sighed. "Let me guess. Which wall have you knocked down now?"

"I haven't knocked down any walls. All fifteen rooms have walls. The library, great room, game room, kitchen, laundry room, both offices, tackle room and—"

"Hold it. What's a tackle room?"

"A room for when I come in from fishing. I need a room for my tackle." He looked serious as he said it until he started laughing. "I needed a couple sinks to gut and clean the fish, too. Not unless she wants me in the kitchen, and I just don't see that happening."

He sounded like the old Lucas now. The fun-loving, happy guy who used to call several times a day seeking Emma's advice. Initially Emma had sounded happy about the house Lucas had been renovating for them in Key West, then she'd come in one day and confessed over a nonfat latte that she wasn't interested in wallpaper swatches and drywall width, so she'd dropped the whole project and his calls into Doreen's lap. Now they talked about everything from wood to wallpaper every day.

Doreen pretended to shiver. "I've seen one fish gutted and I don't ever have to see it again," she said. His laughter conjured up for her sexy, if illicit, images of him. "Go on."

"The formal dining and breakfast rooms are done. Oh, and the master suite is done. One bedroom upstairs is done, but we're still working on the foyer. The floor in the powder room on the main level needs a little work, and of course the other three bedrooms are unfinished. Those are rooms Emma won't want to use right away, but if I have my say…"

He was talking about children, of course. Which Emma had confessed to her just last week she'd never really wanted.

"I'm sure you'll compromise," Doreen said, hating knowing Emma's side while hearing the wistful dreams in Lucas's voice. Doreen couldn't look at him. Who wouldn't want kids with him? She'd grown up alone and had longed for brothers and sisters, if only to fill the loneliness of losing her mother early.

"Doreen, I can practically hear my biological clock ticking."

Laughter snaked out of her like a curl of smoke. "You are out of your mind today, Lucas. What's up with you?"

He groaned. "The question is what's right. Nothing. Must be this Hurricane Ana. Gorgeous name for a woman, but the storm's a real witch. She came through a couple days ago and she's still dogging our island. We need a break. I need some vitamin D, some sunshine, wine and a good woman."

"I've heard the reports, Lucas. But I thought you grew up in Key West. You're not used to the weather down there?"

"I am, but I spent a lot of time in New York as a young man. My father was from Harlem and my mother from the Keys. My father wanted me to be a stockbroker like him. I became one and hated it."

"When did you have time for that and school to become an architect?"

"You have to have a major and a minor," he said, smiling.

"My goodness," she said, impressed. "You must have been some type of genius."

Lucas pretended to straighten a tie he wasn't wearing. "You know I try to tell my best friends, Stephen and Terrence, to bow to my brilliance, but they don't give a damn. They're always telling me to shut up."

Doreen burst out laughing. "Do they beat you up a little, too?"

"They know better."

"So, what's going on with the marble? You never told me. Are you still holding out hope that it will come in? If you are, forget it. It's not too late to go with bamboo. Innovative, right?"

She nervously fingered her hair, hoping he'd take the bait and not want to talk about Emma. Doreen didn't think she could handle a talk about what he should do about her boss.

"More like crazy. Stop worrying. I've got a guy."

Doreen started laughing again. She loved the expression "I've got a guy." Here in the city, having "a guy" usually involved something illegal. "Lucas, I'm hanging up now. I'm not listening to your story about how something fell off the back of a truck."

"Ms. Gamble, I'm appalled at the direction of your thoughts. I would never participate in anything unsavory."

"What about Mo?"

"I plead the Fifth on Mo. I don't know what the hell he does," he said, and they both chuckled. "I thought you wanted to hear about your sink?"

Her sink.

Now that was quite an oxymoron. The sink was no more hers than the house was. She was merely stepping in for her boss. Emma had cringed at the idea of domestication, preferring the big paycheck. She'd been unflinching in her quest for success, practicing her acquired skill set of delegating with executive aplomb.

"Lucas to Doreen," he singsonged when her attention wavered again. "What's with you today?"

"Just thinking of all the things I have to do when I get home. Forgive me. Please tell me about m—the sink."

"Okay." The excitement was all over his face. "The Italian-designed, ceramic-valve construction and polished chrome fit perfectly in that small space. It totally complements the wall coloring you suggested last month."

Lucas's voice had dropped as if he were now reading poetry.

"It's sexy, if I can use that term to describe a bathroom sink. One of the best choices you made for this house."

Joy was one of those emotions Doreen rarely felt, but Lucas's compliment made her feel a deep sense of satisfaction. She could hardly stop herself from floating out of her West Forty-Fourth Street window. Doreen planted her cheek on her hand. "You flatter me. Please, make me feel good some more."

"When you say it like that, I feel obligated to tell you that I'm promised to another woman—but if I weren't, I'd take you up on your offer."

Doreen couldn't believe that a tiny scream leapt out of her mouth. Lucas's voice had struck the right note at the heart of her loneliness. "I'd better go. I believe that I have a brain leak that needs to be plugged with food and sleep."

"No harm done," he said, laughing.

Doreen put her hand over the webcam to experience the full bloom of embarrassment. Could she humiliate herself any further?

Lucas was so cool about everything, but she needed to sever these evening talks. All of her friends had said so. Doreen took her hand off the camera and stood up, the nonverbal cue that a meeting was over. "No harm except to my ego," she admitted. "Have a good night, Lucas."

"Hey, don't go. We're cool, okay? I still haven't gotten my furniture yet."

He didn't want to hang up. Damn Emma!

Doreen shook her head, locking her knees, making herself remain standing. "You have lawn chairs. Bring them inside and watch your too-big television and eat off paper plates."

"Now you're being cruel. They're reinforced cardboard or something."

"Only the best for you," she said, the marquee down the street flashing the start time of *The Color Purple*.

"I need to speak to Emma. Is she around?"

Doreen looked over her shoulder to her boss's closed door and shook her head. "No, she's in a meeting. I'll leave a note for her to call you, okay?"

"Doreen, I hope I didn't offend you earlier."

"No. I have guy friends and they tease me all the time." *Liar.* She straightened her already-tidy desk, willing her legs to relax before she got a charley horse.

"Good," he said, unaware of the lingering pain she felt at not having a man for herself. But that wasn't his business. "Emma knew I was calling, right?"

She felt as if he was right next to her. "Yes, I gave her your message this morning."

"And her schedule was clear at that time."

Doreen bit her lip, saying nothing. As big as her crush was, she couldn't tell him that Emma had reviewed the message on her computer and deleted it within seconds. Doreen couldn't say that. She wished he couldn't even see her.

"I need to speak to her right now. I need to know what time to pick her up from the airport tomorrow." He said it as if it were a challenge she could promptly rise to meet.

Doreen's fingers quickly flew across the keyboard, accessing Emma's schedule. She hadn't known anything about Emma going to Florida this weekend. As far as she knew, her boss was scheduled to go to the annual sales meeting in the Poconos.

"Lucas, can I have her call you back? I can't disturb her right now. In fact, I was just leaving."

Lying to him wasn't what she wanted to do, but she didn't want to get fired for crossing the line of professionalism.

In truth, she'd been waiting for Emma to discuss the new job listing of director of special events that had just been posted. They'd talked about it months ago, when they'd gotten word that the position was being created, but Emma had been tight-lipped lately. Doreen hadn't minded being her assistant when Emma was the director of promotions, but she'd just been promoted to vice president, and her new position would take her to the corporate office where an administrative assistant would be provided, so Doreen would have to make the adjustment to a new boss or become a boss herself.

If she hadn't already been doing the job, maybe she wouldn't have felt so strongly about applying, but she knew everything it entailed and she was up for the challenge.

No, now was not the time to go where this conversation with Lucas was heading. Lately his discontent was becoming more apparent, and Doreen didn't want to be in the middle of his crumbling relationship with Emma. Neither seemed to be aware of the direction it was heading in, and Doreen didn't want to play marriage counselor. She was single for a reason.

"It's nearly seven-thirty, and you're still there, Dorie." Calling her by the nickname he'd coined ratcheted up her guilt like a crane with a bar of girded steel. Doreen felt caught in the middle of a lovers' quarrel, except she didn't know what the fight was about.

"Lucas, I'm sorry. I don't know what's happening here."

"I've left messages and she hasn't returned my calls. We make plans for the house and she doesn't follow through. Since I can't get her on the phone—" He paused and Doreen waited a beat too long.

"This may be the last message you have to deliver. Tell Emma if she doesn't come to Florida tomorrow, I'll consider us over." Then he hung up.

Chapter 2

Lucas could have kicked himself before he fully pushed the disconnect button.

"Doreen? Doreen?" Why had he involved Doreen in his and Emma's relationship problems? It wasn't her fault that he was a failure at having—or *not* having—a fiancée.

Before he made another mistake, he tried to think things through. In the past he'd been quick to think the worst of women when they didn't call, or if they called too much; if they didn't stay, or if they wanted to stay. If they drank, or if they didn't drink.

During the past five years, he'd just about driven himself crazy wondering what women wanted from men. And then he started listening to his DJ friend Terrence. As crazy as he had been in the past with his off-the-wall ideas about relationships, the brother now made sense, and Lucas tuned in to his radio show whenever he had the chance.

According to Terrence, women wanted good men who treated them like they were worth something. But a man had to be selective, too. He had to choose carefully, because there were some crazy ladies out there.

Lucas thought about how he'd found Emma in New York. His company had won the contract to renovate three floors of the office building she worked in. He'd seen her for a couple weeks going to her boss's office for a meeting, and then one day he approached her. They'd dated happily for months, and then he accepted another renovation project in Key West, his mother's hometown.

Emma had assured him dating long distance wouldn't be a problem, as long as they were committed. She'd been all for it for the first two years, but in these last eight months, their relationship had all but evaporated like some of the local lakes.

He'd ignored the signs, and his fading love for her, hoping she'd come around and still want to move to Key West like she'd promised, so they could be together and rekindle their true feelings for each other. This weekend was the test. If she came, he'd told himself, they'd live happily ever after.

If she didn't show up, they'd go their separate ways.

The next day, Lucas hammered nails into the roof.

Terrence was right. When a woman didn't call you back, somebody else was probably occupying her mind and her time.

Lucas descended from the roof to check on his

foreman, Mo, who was installing granite flooring in the foyer and lower bathroom. He stayed outside on the porch, his hands on the white siding as he leaned into the house. Only Mo and Rog were allowed to enter through the front door while the granite was being installed. The materials were too expensive and delicate.

Mo looked up and followed a carefully laid path of crisscrossed boards that never touched the foyer floor.

Lucas grasped his foreman's hand and pulled him out of the house. "How's it coming?"

They leaned in like spies. "Good," Mo replied. "This needs to dry for four more hours, and then we'll come back and redo any areas that show unevenness. Everything is cut to perfection, even the corners. Looks easy, doesn't it?"

Mo was a big Mexican man who'd been born in America. He knew how to build a house better than anyone Lucas had ever met. More than that, he knew great craftsmanship.

Lucas nodded. "It does, but will it be ready in time?"

As they talked, Rog never stopped working. The Italian craftsman had been in the country for six months, working with an outfit that had suddenly gone out of business, stranding him. He'd been doing day labor when Mo had snapped him up. His work was flawless.

Lucas tipped back his baseball cap and scratched his head. "Tomorrow is the magic hour. Will this be ready?"

Mo consulted Rog. They discussed everything in Italian, one of the three languages Mo spoke. Lucas knew only about two hundred words of Spanish, so he was lost.

He looked toward heaven. He needed for everything to be perfect. His relationship with Emma had been far from it. In fact, lately they'd had no relationship at all, and he was concerned that after all this effort for her to like everything in the house, he'd be the one to call their wedding off.

Mo told him what he wanted to hear. "We'll be ready, if I pick up his wife and two daughters from the airport." He looked like he'd bitten into a bad apple.

Lucas extended his hand to Rog, laughing at Mo. "Excellent."

Rog shook his hand and then kissed Lucas on both cheeks. Mo hurried down the stairs before he was the recipient of Rog's affection.

"Ciao." Rog rushed back to work as Lucas wiped his face off with his sleeve, Mo laughing from the sidewalk.

"He drives me crazy when he does that," Mo told him. "I try to stay away from him. He cries a lot, too."

"And you don't? Every time Armella and the kids leave, you're a waterspout."

"Hey! Don't say that too loud. The men won't respect me," Mo said, looking around to see if anyone had heard Lucas.

They checked on the progress of the workers whose job it was to clean up the property after Hurricane Ana. It had come through as a Category One a couple days ago and rumbled out to sea, but in a freak turn of events, it seemed to reverse direction and was once again taking aim on south Florida. The I-10 had been reopened this morning and traffic had resumed, but the storm would be back wreaking havoc once again in a couple days.

In fact, dark clouds already clung to the horizon.

As if he read his mind, Mo said, "This storm smells like trouble."

"Don't be a pessimist." Lucas waited a few seconds. "Emma's coming tomorrow."

"Is that why you look like you got caught with your hand in the candy jar? The airport opened up?"

"I did something, but not that bad, and yes, the airport is open. All those people need to be recycled." Lucas tried to laugh. He felt anxious knowing Emma was coming, yet she still hadn't called. Doreen hadn't called back, either. He guessed she'd given up and gone home. He would have, and let him and Emma deal with their own problems.

The workers tossed onto the ground plywood that had been used during the last storms. Much of it had disintegrated from too much water.

"Lucas, how honest can I be with you?" Mo said, his Spanish accent sounding musical. He was about to share some wisdom.

Lucas eyed his friend. "You want to get paid today?"

"Okay," Mo said, "straight up. You haven't seen her in a long time. Eight months. The house isn't finished and you're not a raving lunatic. You would think you'd want everything to be perfect. Do you care?"

Caught off guard, Lucas considered his question. "Yeah. You saw me pressing Rog."

"Our talk was a little more extensive. I promised him a few things for the family. It'll cost you about a hundred dollars. You have to pick them up while I run to the airport. I'll make a list."

Lucas snorted good-naturedly. "The bastard."

Both men chuckled.

"All I'm saying is when you first got here from New York, I had to institute a 'no cell phone' rule on the job."

Lucas smiled.

"You stepped off the roof eave backwards, fell half a story and separated your shoulder. You fell through the floor at the Wilcox mall refurbishment, requiring an ambulance and fifteen stitches. I don't know how a nail was shot through your index finger, but that was a lot of paperwork and a hospital visit."

"That shouldn't count," Lucas argued halfheartedly. "That extern from the technical school shot me from across the room."

"But if you hadn't been on the phone with Emma you'd have seen him playing with the nail gun. Since you and Emma have cooled it," Mo went on, "we've had no accidents."

Lucas couldn't argue with the truth. "You're very observant," he finally said.

"That's why you pay me the big bucks." Mo wiped his hair back and put his cap back in place, shielding the skin around his eyes that looked like it was made from cracked glass.

They walked to the back of the property, finding nails in the grass and pitching them into buckets along the walkway.

Mo's daughter had stepped on a nail last year on Take Your Daughter to Work Day. Since then, the men cleaned up after themselves.

Lucas and Mo leaned against the back fence, admiring the gray house with the pink accent shutters.

"I gave Emma an ultimatum: be on the plane tomorrow or it's over."

Mo looked as if he'd tasted something sour. "You're not too bright today, huh?"

"First you say I don't care, and now I'm not smart?"

They gathered up the old shutters the workers had taken down and loaded them into the back of the pickup.

"Lucas, you can't issue an ultimatum to a woman and expect her to give you food and sex."

"I didn't give it to her. I told Doreen."

"Her assistant? You just officially crossed over into wimp territory."

"Emma hasn't returned my calls."

"Dude, do I have to explain what that means in women's language?"

"No."

Mo just shook his head as Lucas picked up the street sign he'd knocked down and dragged it inside the gate to deal with later.

Once they were done for the day, Lucas went inside and dialed Emma's number. All he got was a message that her voice mail was full.

Everything that had and hadn't transpired between them over the last eight months came flooding back. The promises that she'd come down to Key West, his disappointment when she hadn't. His messages asking her to call him, her failure to phone back. The cancelled trips, Emma's emotional distance and his nonchalance about it, their missed phone calls, their tendency to mainly communicate via voice mail.

Before he could hang up he was transferred to Doreen's voice mail. "This is Doreen Gamble. I'm away from my desk, but if it's important you can page me at 5546, or leave me a message, and I'll get back to you right away."

He had no doubt that she'd call him back.

Her voice was as warm and welcoming as her smile and he'd taken advantage of her. Lucas's first inclination was to page her, but he didn't. He needed to settle things with Emma. The beep sounded in his ear, and he took a breath to speak, though he didn't know what to say.

"You deserve better than this," he said, and hung up before "I'm sorry" could come out.

He'd have to do it when he was thinking clearly. Maybe tomorrow. Just not today.

Doreen waited patiently for Emma to finish her conversation with the president of Regents Cable. For having been promoted only a month ago, she was confident and personable with the head honcho.

"Yes, Jeffrey, I'll be glad to attend the network meeting with you next month. I'm honored you chose me." She nodded her head as if he could see her and smiled brightly, giving Doreen the thumbs-up, her new symbolic gesture of success. Doreen just hoped she didn't do that at the Black Greek convention. They'd skewer her.

Emma had made it. She'd moved on up, as the old saying went.

Shaquemma Rowena Johnson had been born and bred in Brooklyn, had attended State University of

New York at Buffalo, and had graduated with a degree in communications. She'd worked her way up through the ranks of three networks and two cable companies.

In seventeen years since college graduation she'd shed her heavy accent, thick eyebrows and overbearing attitude, and had polished, injected and dieted away all other unseemly features.

She'd studied women of power, and now she was the one wearing the expensive suit, carrying the top-of-the-line Louis Vuitton briefcase, having power lunches. She was now legally Emma Jones, a woman to be reckoned with.

Emma hung up her phone, caressing the black receiver with her fingertip.

Without looking up at Doreen she said, "I need you to go to Key West and end my engagement to Lucas."

Doreen blinked at her. "What?"

"Break up with Lucas and I'll give you five extra days of vacation."

"He's expecting you to be there tomorrow." All the respect Doreen had for Emma was sucked up by Greta's vacuum cleaner as she moved by the executive's outer door.

Emma glanced at her iPhone and pouted for a fraction of a second. "I'm not going to Florida. You already knew that. I'm heading to the Poconos. Do this for me, and you can write your own ticket. Do you understand what that means, Doreen? This is how business is done." She folded her hands and finally looked up. "Within reason, what would you like that I can do for you?"

It was August, and suddenly Doreen felt like she was being treated to an early Christmas she didn't deserve. Though her heart raced at the idea of meeting Lucas face-to-face, she couldn't under these circumstances. "Lucas loves you, Emma."

Her lips popped out again. "No, he doesn't. He loves what he thinks we have, but it's not true. Lucas wants that more than anything. I'm too selfish for him. The last eight months have taught me a lot about myself. Besides, Lucas changed the rules. When I met him he was living up here and was a successful architect and builder, but after his job he moved back, and I understood. His business was growing by leaps and bounds there, but New York still has a lot to offer. His heart is in Florida with his mother and his friends, but mine isn't.

"Over time I thought I'd change my mind, but I haven't. It's too bad because he's a good man. But at my level, I can get one of any race, any age." She shrugged as if that was all there was to getting a man.

"Ten days vacation," Emma then offered, the heartfelt, melancholy woman of seconds ago gone. "Do you feel better?"

Doreen hated to admit that she did. "Marginally."

Doreen decided not to make this easy. Emma would be gone soon, and extra vacation days under a new manager could easily be reversed. No, she wanted more.

"Emma, months ago you said you'd recommend me for the new position of director of special events. I'd like to move forward with that now."

"Mmm." Emma twisted her hands and her lips. "I'm

not so sure you'd get it going from being my assistant. Dream a little smaller."

Doreen's skin began to crawl. How dare she all but promise her the job, and now try to weasel out of it? And who'd told Shaquemma Rowena Johnson to dream small?

Doreen got up and headed for the door. "Good night, Emma."

At Emma's slow clap, Doreen turned. Their office was across from the Broadway theatres, but the theatrics in the office were overplayed. "I'm glad to see you have tenacity. That's what the job needs. I'll be glad to recommend you. Meet Lucas in the baggage claim area by the carousel."

Doreen didn't turn around and kept her hand on the door.

"I'll wait five minutes for your glowing written recommendation, and then I'll go to Key West and take care of this for you." Doreen finally turned around.

The fact that Emma was impressed showed in her quirked lip. "You've been doing your homework. Very good."

Doreen's heart broke for Lucas. "I had a good teacher. I'll need your credit card to make the reservations."

"It's already on your desk."

Chapter 3

Doreen held her stomach as it pitched during the bumpy landing. The bagel and cream cheese she'd eaten before takeoff now felt like a Michelin tire in her stomach.

Nerves were getting the best of her. She didn't like being the bearer of bad news or flying in rainstorms.

But a much larger problem loomed as voluminous as the clouds that suffocated the Florida sky. She hadn't broken up with a man since college, almost ten years ago. She'd been really cocky last night with Emma, but in the soggy light of day, she'd stared into her mirror and saw her unlined, amber-colored eyes, and the chicken in them was real.

How was she going to tell Lucas, a man she secretly crushed on, that his relationship with Emma was over?

Oh, and it was nice building this house with you long distance. Goodbye.

This morning when she'd gotten up, she'd still been angry at Emma, and even now the anger simmered within her. She wanted to cry, but all she could do was squeeze out a throat-burning burp. Doreen pushed her fingers into a steeple formation around her forehead while she stared at the floor.

What were the appropriate words to end another's engagement?

I'm sorry, but Emma doesn't love you anymore.

Emma sent me to break up with you.

Emma's an idiot.

Oh, and by the way, I have a crush on you.

All of it was just wrong.

The plane bounced as it landed and taxied to the gate, and her stomach gurgled loud enough for the lady across the aisle to glance at her sympathetically. She watched the rain slant against the window, then unbuckled her seat belt and stood with the rest of the passengers.

She retrieved her computer from the overhead compartment and silently waved goodbye to her luxurious accommodations in first class. If Emma wasn't going to clean up her own mess, she was at least going to pay for a first-class garbage cleaner.

Lucas watched Doreen in the two-piece black suit circle the baggage carousel, knowing she wasn't his fiancée, but had been dispatched by her. New York women wore black as if it were prescribed by a physician exclusively for them.

She was tall with a face like Vanessa Williams, except her color was a few shades deeper, reminding him of honey. She had an amazing body, curvy in places women were meant to be; soft and slim in all the right places, too. Her hair reminded him of summers in the Keys, with the way it hung down and breezed airily over her shoulder as she searched the airport. She looked down and saw the unmoving baggage carousel; her hand slid up to her neck and she stepped back, resting her weight on her left foot, hand on her hip.

He was disappointed because his engagement was over, but he couldn't help but feel he'd been granted a reprieve. One thing he did not understand: why didn't the loss seem greater?

Still he watched Doreen. Her collar was open, and she caressed her neck as she perused the baggage claim area and consulted her watch. Men noticed her, but she was oblivious to them, her actions indicating her schedule was tight. She kept reading a card she took out and reinserted into her pocket repeatedly. Was she practicing what she was going to say to him on behalf of Emma? Apparently this wasn't a game to her.

Finally the last of his heart broke with a clap of thunder.

Doreen's back bowed and he stepped out of the shadows.

He was no longer engaged, and he needed to let his ex-fiancée's assistant know that he knew.

Lucas put his hands in his jeans pockets as he walked up behind Doreen, who was digging for her phone. "You don't have to call me. I'm here."

Doreen turned around, her mouth kissable and open. She closed her eyes and shook her head. "She's not coming, Lucas. I'm—I'm here to break up with you for her. I'm so sorry."

The baggage carousel surged behind her and she turned to watch. Lucas wasn't one for mystical or symbolic signs, but his mother would have said that meant to move on. Why wasn't he surprised?

He shook his head. This was so Emma. They were so wrong in what they'd done to themselves and, more important, to Doreen. Who exactly did they think they were? Hollywood celebrities?

He touched Doreen's arm and she looked at his hand, then his eyes.

"We haven't officially met, but I feel like I know you already. Lucas McCoy. Terrible way to meet, but it is what it is."

"You do know me, Lucas," she said, touching his hand. "I'm so sorry." She then did an unexpected thing: she hugged him.

Instinct made him hug her back, but the man in him enjoyed the feel of a woman who genuinely wanted to comfort him. He caught his breath and let his mind race back over the last months to all the signs he should have paid attention to. All the questions he should have asked. The additional trips to New York he should have taken. He needed to officially end things with Emma.

Doreen stepped back.

"There," she said, looking embarrassed. "At least I feel a bit better. I'm still sorry, though."

"Don't apologize unless this was your idea."

Her smile was quick. "It definitely wasn't."

"Emma and I should have had a conversation on the phone and saved a whole lot of money."

"Sometimes those conversations are the hardest ones to have, Lucas. I guess that's why she couldn't come. I'm not making excuses for her. I'm suggesting that she just couldn't say the words."

Doreen shrugged and turned to look at the luggage. Her hair was gorgeous as it swung well past her shoulders, cut into a shagged V, ending between her shoulder blades. The cut didn't make sense to him, but it looked good.

"You expecting a bag?" he asked.

"I am."

"So you're the bearer of bad news? This in your job description?"

Pain seemed to shoot up her right cheek and end in her forehead. All of the muscles moved and she stopped them with her fingers, and he was sorry he asked.

"Yes, it is."

"What color is your suitcase?"

"Red."

"Not black? That's good. Easier to spot." He shoved his hands in his pockets. He wasn't usually so sarcastic. He searched for another line of conversation, but he decided that silence in the midst of the airport noise was better.

Her bag popped up, and like a New York woman Doreen reached past businessmen and wrestled her bag off the conveyer. Men stepped to the side, some acting scared, others laughing. She ignored them and him.

"Doreen, let me get it." Lucas eased it from her hands. "How long are you intending to stay?"

"I have a flight out tonight, but I thought perhaps we'd have time for a bite and I could see the house."

"First thing's first. Leaving tonight isn't going to happen. While you were flying down, all of the flights going out for today were canceled. You see that long line over there?" Lucas pointed to the row of people snaking up and down like the security check-in line.

"Yes." She looked crestfallen, her mouth hanging open.

"That's for flight reservations to get out of here."

"That's terrible." She looked even more uncomfortable. Her black bag slipped down her shoulder and landed in her fingers. She looked like she was thinking of her next move. "I need to get back."

"Not happening tonight. Let me borrow your phone."

Lucas dialed Emma's number and she picked up immediately. "How'd he take it?"

His heart didn't skip a beat as it had earlier when reality had set in. It hadn't yesterday or last month. His body didn't go through any of the physical transformations it used to at the sound of her voice. None of the reactions happened that used to happen, and he knew they were over. He hadn't heard her voice in two weeks, and for a second he wished their end could have been different, but they'd been over for a while and nothing would change that.

"I'm taking our breakup just fine, Emma. It would have been better if you'd just come out and told me, though."

Doreen walked off and he appreciated her discretion.

"I'm sorry, Lucas."

"Yeah, me, too. Why couldn't you just tell me it wasn't working for you?"

"I don't know. I didn't want to get into an argument. I could ask you the same thing." There was no accusation in her voice, just a bit of melancholy.

"I'd hoped we could have fixed whatever was broken this weekend."

"I'm not a piece of wood that can be crafted. We would have had a chance if you'd stayed up here, but you chose to go to Key West."

"You're right. But work took me up there to New York and brought me back here. Had you not agreed to come here, I wouldn't have started with you," he said gently. "This is the last thing I wanted." His family was so small. Just him and his mother. While she was alive, he wanted to be near her.

"I know, sweetheart."

She relented her tough New York stance, the ball-breaking woman she'd sometimes become when she had to have her way. He'd loved to watch her move between both worlds, though she'd done it rarely the last few times he'd seen her. Lucas blamed himself. He should have known then she was making a permanent change. He doubted he'd ever see this side of Emma again—if he ever saw her again.

"I know your business is important, and your mom," she said. "You know I don't need my family, and I didn't mind the idea of moving away from them, but it's New York I'd miss."

"You're a hustler, baby. You love your job, the pace of the city, and the wheeling and dealing. Key West is too sedate for you."

"NYC is in me, Lucas." Emma laughed softly and he joined her. "Just like I know it's not in you."

"Come on, now. I liked New York well enough," he said. "But there comes a time when you have to follow your priorities. Money isn't everything. Family, love, all mean something to me."

"We hadn't had love for a while. I never had the guts to ask you to come back here when it wasn't in your heart, Lucas. I just hoped you'd want to and you never did. If you're honest, you'll find out you stopped loving me a while ago, but honor made kept you pursuing our relationship. Now I'm going to let you go."

"Wait." He sighed her name softly. People were coming in from the rain, but he focused on none. "I'm sorry, Emma."

"Me too. I'll never forget you." Her voice cracked. "You're a really good man."

He turned, looking at Doreen and her brown high-lighted hair. Crouched over her bag, she pulled out a coat and was unzipping compartments in search of something else. Every minute or two she'd scoot up to keep up in line. Why was she in the car-rental line anyway?

He pulled himself back to his phone conversation. "Listen, Emma. No more flights are going out tonight, so Doreen will be here overnight. Maybe a couple nights, depending on the hurricane." He rubbed his eyes, ready to hang up and drink a beer to forget this day.

"No problem. Tell her to call when she's on her way home."

"Okay. Well, I guess this is where we part." Lucas dropped his head to end the call privately.

"Goodbye, Lucas." The words still hurt just a little.

"Bye, Emma."

As Lucas ended the call, thunder clapped so loud people in the crowd ducked, including Doreen.

"We'd better get going," he said, handing her the phone. "It's over. Thanks, Doreen."

"I'm sorry." She looked around. Everywhere but at him. "You can leave me," she said. "I need to make a hotel reservation."

"You can stay at the house. There's more than enough room."

He'd seen her happy and now she'd lost her glow. Now that her job was done, she seemed lost. "I don't want to impose, Lucas."

Lucas grabbed her bag, her words raising his ire. He turned around and Doreen bumped right into him. "Ow, sorry," she said, so close he could smell the mint from her gum.

He steadied her but didn't let her go. "You're not imposing, it's not a bother, and I don't want to hear any more about it. You were in the wrong line anyway. All of those people," he said, as he gestured to another line of people that had wrapped around a bank of phones, "are waiting to make hotel arrangements. You're in the car-rental line."

Her gaze ricocheted from the line, the signage and back to his. Thunder boomed again and she shook. He moved closer to let a skycap by with a cart full of un-claimed luggage.

Her breasts grazed his chest and her hands slid up his arms. "That's so loud."

Lucas didn't move. God wasn't being cruel. Life had just dealt him a fair hand. He hadn't felt breasts in eight months. "Don't tell me you're scared of a little thunder." Lucas almost didn't believe her. But this was Doreen. The woman who'd walked in a marathon for breast cancer because a friend of a friend had suffered with the disease and she'd wanted to help.

He waited for the familiar sizzle of lightning and she shivered and nearly covered her ears in response to more thunder. "Sounds like the building is being demolished."

She looked up as if she half expected something to fall from the sky. Each time thunder rumbled, she sucked in her lips and shook just a little. She wasn't going to like it down here. Lucas grabbed the bag again, watching her.

"Born and raised a city girl, right?" He carefully stepped away from Doreen and guided her to the short-term hourly parking lot and his truck. He placed the luggage in the bed, secured the covering and held her door while she got in.

"Small town in New York State called Oswego. I told you before, I used to go to my grandmother's house every summer in North Carolina. But I never got used to the storms. Now I go to a friend's house so I'm not by myself." She looked at the grayish sky with concern.

It struck him that there wasn't any pretentiousness about Doreen. She was honest about her fear and he didn't feel right teasing her like he would have Emma. He'd have to be gentler with Doreen.

He got in and coasted to the automated exit, paid the fee and accessed the highway before taking an early exit and driving through the residential streets.

The first thing he noticed was that Doreen didn't have an open magazine on her lap like Emma would have. Doreen was looking at the houses, muttering that she liked this or that. She rolled her window down even though a light mist fell from the sky.

"That is so sweet," she declared, pointing as they drove by a small, weather-worn white house. "How much do you think it's going for?"

He'd checked into the house for investment purposes just a week ago. "Just short of a million dollars. Nine twenty-nine, to be exact."

"No! Slow down. I need to see that again. What's inside?"

"Two tiny bedrooms and one bathroom still decorated in the seventies green and yellow. Been in the same family for four decades."

He drove on and had to wipe the dopey grin off his face before she saw it.

"They're crazy. They might get three hundred thousand, but not a penny more."

He couldn't tell her they'd already received three full-price offers.

"What took you to New York City?" he asked.

"An internship with Regents Cable. I worked for a few different companies and then Regents called. They had an excellent educational program that paid for me to get a degree, so I went back to school. Things are finally falling into place and I'm being promoted to director of special events."

"Is work all you do? Isn't there someone special in your life?"

She looked kind of wary. They'd never ventured into this territory before. Before, they'd been protected by the rules of his engagement to Emma. Now their status was different.

"There isn't anyone, but I'm happy."

Her gaze was intelligent and assessing. He felt like he was on one of the court shows his mother was fond of watching when she was home. Right now, she was in Cairo, sightseeing and having the time of her life, no doubt.

"If I'm getting too personal, just let me know."

Doreen crossed her left leg over her right. "I'm letting you know."

Lucas took a mental step back. "All right, city girl. I'll leave you alone."

"Thank you."

The unapologetic stop sign had been thrust into his face, halting his forward trajectory down the road of her personal life.

There was time, he knew, but everything was happening at breakneck speed, and for some reason he felt the need to know so much about her. But he didn't rush. He was sorry he pressed Doreen.

The silence stretched as he drove the back roads, cutting through the residential neighborhoods he loved to scout.

"That blue house looks familiar. I know that sounds ridiculous because I've never been here before, but the white spindles on the front porch, the picket fence leading to the curb... Is that the first house you renovated?"

How long ago had he described that house to her? Seven, no, eight months ago? How many conversations had they had since then? He looked at the house and pushed back his baseball cap.

"That's the one. You have an incredible memory."

"Are the owners still there or was it resold?"

"No, they're still there. He's a former mayor and she was a state senator of Ohio. My guys built them a garage last month."

"Too small a job for you?"

"No, I was finishing my house."

"Right. Sorry." The tension in Doreen's face was etched around her mouth and forehead. "What's that clicking sound?"

Lucas pulled over and shut off the engine. "Just wait a couple seconds and look in that direction."

"It sounds like a herd of horses."

"When have you ever heard a herd of horses?" he teased.

"On TV."

"Just watch. Listen." He touched her shoulder, his fingers grazing her soft dark hair. A man could easily learn to love holding the strands all night long.

Just as the thought shocked him, the rain had the same effect on her. It stormed up the block like the infamous running of the bulls, overpowering the truck, thumping the roof, causing her to flinch. Her shoulder bumped his and he chuckled.

Doreen punched him in the thigh.

"What did I do?" he protested.

"You're laughing at me."

"You should see your face. You look like a kid. Like you've never seen rain before."

"I've seen it, but I've never heard it like this before." They sat there for a few minutes as she watched it rain all around them. "I feel vulnerable out here. I left New York and it was a beautiful day, and now I'm trapped here and I can't leave. I feel as if I'm not safe."

For a second she'd scratched his leg with her nails, but now she held her hands in her lap.

This wasn't a case of hysterics. Her fear was contained but just beneath the surface.

The clouds were ominous and the tide high. The storm promised to be strong and it could turn deadly at any time. Hurricane Ana had already proved herself to be formidable and had drifted back out to sea. No one wished for her return, but the Weather Service predicted she'd make landfall again in a couple days.

Lucas looked at Doreen, whose eyes reminded him of the time he'd been in Africa and had seen liquid gold flecked with tidbits of coal. He'd seen nothing more beautiful.

"I won't let anything happen to you," he told her. He knew his reassurance might not hold much weight, but she was here because of him. He had to help her get through this.

Doreen didn't believe him. She folded her arms

across her chest, her neck tilted and her eyebrow quirked up on the end. Words were unnecessary.

"Let's just get to the house, Lucas, and tomorrow your babysitting job will be over."

This was the first crack in her facade. "Hey." He unbuckled his seat belt and slid across the seat. "Come on now. I promise not to let anything bad happen to you. All right?" Some of the tension eased from her body and she looked at him and then away. "Are we friends again?"

"Maybe," she said, and he got the impression she didn't want to hurt his feelings by calling him a liar to his face.

"Can I hug you? A tiny hug? I'm not trying to feel you up for free or anything."

She laughed a little, her hands gripping the seat. He wanted her to trust him.

"Please?" he asked.

"Okay," she said, and to his surprise she reached over and hugged him.

"Oh, my God," he whispered. "I'm never going to want to stop holding you."

"Lucas!" She was playing again.

Even with her protest, he still didn't let her go for another few seconds, then reluctantly, he slid over and started the truck. This was the Doreen he knew. Always getting on him for something. "All right, we're going. But you've got to promise we'll do that again."

She laughed, sounding more like herself. "I really do think you have a mental illness."

"Why? Because I complimented your hugging ability? You don't hug like a cute girl, with your butt stuck out and a pat on the back. Somebody knows they've been touched when they hug you. That's really good."

"Thanks," she said, a sincere smile blooming on her face.

Thunder rumbled. "I better get to the hardware store before you have to swim back to New York. You look like you're tired of Florida and you've only been here thirty minutes."

"Swim? I don't know how to swim. I began learning, but never finished. I need a refresher course."

Her expression was so cute he could tell she was serious, although she was smiling.

"A refresher course." He nodded. "Not sure they offer those, but you could just get in the water and start stroking."

"I could try that."

Thunder boomed and she jumped off the seat, her hands shooting up. "My goodness. I have to stop that."

"You sure do." He laughed. "You're about to scare me to death and I'll kill somebody." Lucas looked at her, then at the road. Then at her again. "You're too old to be screaming."

"Lucas McCoy, how are you telling me I'm too old for something? I didn't say that to you last month when you told me you chased down that ice cream truck, did I?"

"There's my friend Doreen."

She rolled her eyes and acted like she wasn't going to smile at him. "Did you order some thunder to get the real me to come out?"

"As a matter of fact, I did."

"You're full of it. You didn't know I was coming."

"There's that New York woman I've been missing. Florida women are so Southern and sweet. New York women are mean and hard." He pumped his fist at her and she playfully hit his hand. "See what I mean? You're mean as hell."

"I don't want to be mean to you. I don't know how to be." The words settled between them. "We need to talk, Lucas."

He drove awhile. "And we will. Let's give it a minute to settle in. Do you like hip hop or jazz?"

"Both." Her nails were polished this pretty pink color, and he liked that. This was the land of white-tipped nails and shih tzu dogs and year-round tans. Doreen, however, was an original.

He pressed the button on the radio. "This station plays a little of both at different times of the day. The DJ—Holy Terror—is one of my best friends. His real name is Terrence Jeffries. Used to play for the Dolphins. He's hard on women, but he means well, and he's funny."

"We've got some real characters in New York, too. But you already know that."

Lucas turned down the volume. "You're right. Let's go ahead and clear the air. I don't want what happened between Emma and me to affect what happens while you're here."

She looked uneasy. "I don't want to know about your relationship. I worked for her, and that essentially ended today. It's a formality once I get back, but she'll have already moved into her new office with her new assistant, Carl."

"All the better," he said.

Assessing and direct, she stared him down. "What does that mean?"

"It means that whatever happens this weekend, you won't feel obligated to report to Emma. She won't pressure you into telling her what went on, and you won't feel as if you have to navigate between two worlds. You're not obligated to play the straight man for both of us. I'm sorry I even put you in that situation."

"Oh." A sweep of her hand sent her hair behind her ear. Silver hoop earrings slid into view.

"Now that's it's over between Emma and me, you can tell me if she said anything bad about me."

She exhaled through her nose and intentionally blinked at him. "Lucas." The way she said his name made him laugh. A thin line between patience and trouble. And she was short on patience.

He started laughing. "I'm just kidding. All you said was 'Oh.' I was expecting something else. Like 'Thank God,' or 'I'm so glad I don't have to listen to you two anymore.' But 'Oh'? It's kind of a letdown, to be honest."

Exasperation and relief seemed to make her shake her head. "Aren't you supposed to be going somewhere?"

"Now you want to get bossy and evil."

"Just drive before you get into more trouble."

"Yes, ma'am."

"Is it really over?" Doreen asked.

"Yes."

"How do you know?"

"Because we don't love each other anymore," he explained as he turned to look at her. Over her shoulder he noticed the drains were full and made a mental note to call Stephen and report the blockage. Stephen Morales was not only one of his best friends, but also the deputy sheriff. He didn't chance driving. Not now while his life was swirling with the water, spinning in a new direction.

"Then why did you want Emma to come down here so badly?" Doreen asked him.

"To work out our problems. I don't believe in giving anything up easily. I have no siblings and only a mother left. I don't want you to feel sorry for me, but I believe in trying to work out things that I start. If she had come down here, I would have asked her to stay."

"I have a huge adopted family—"

"You're lucky," he broke in, wistful. "I'm sorry. That's something I've always wanted. My mom's away right now, but she's the reason I live in Key West. While she's alive, I want to be with her. Emma isn't attached to her family. She doesn't have a relationship with them at all. That was important to me."

"Did she know that?" Doreen held up her hand. "Of course she did. If you're telling me, you told her."

"You know I did, but that's all right. I feel a sense of relief."

"No sadness, Lucas? I know I would feel a sense of loss or something."

Lucas started the car and pulled away from the curb. There *was* a sense of loss. He'd built a house for a woman he'd thought he'd share a life with. "I'd be an unfeeling bastard if I didn't feel anything. But it's not as if I didn't see the writing on the wall." He drove in silence for a while.

"You seem so settled about everything yesterday. I thought you were going to take my head off."

"Doreen, I was wrong for that. Really wrong. It wasn't your responsibility to field our personal calls and referee our discussions. That shouldn't have ever happened. That won't ever happen again."

"How do you know?"

"Because the woman I get with will never get tired of talking to me."

Doreen's fingers plowed through her hair and she tilted her head. He knew that move. She didn't believe him. "And you know this how?" she asked.

"Because I won't get tired of talking to her. I've got to change, too. I realize that now. Our relationship is over and the love is gone, but maybe that wouldn't have happened if I'd given her some alternatives. I'll know for the next time. And there definitely will be a next time."

Chapter 4

Where Doreen was emotional over personal decisions, Lucas was decisive. Maybe that was why relationships had been challenging for her in the past, Doreen thought. Lucas's epiphany startled her, but she settled into the seat knowing that she wouldn't have let distance keep her away from a good man like him.

Letting the stress ease from her body, Doreen studied Lucas, comparing his features to what she'd seen on the webcam. The camera hadn't done him justice. He was a handsome man, his face smooth and brown like dark sugar, his hair soft, curly and black. His baseball cap seemed to be as much a part of him as his T-shirt and sunglasses, which he wore attached to a thick string around his neck, even though there was no hint of sun in the sky.

Like all handsome men, he had long dark eyelashes that fluttered when he smiled, and she found herself wanting to see that wide grin and feel his laugh run all over her skin.

The one thing she'd adored on men were full lips, and Lucas's mouth seemed to invite kisses. She sighed and when he looked at her, she looked away, not wanting to get caught staring. But she had been enjoying the view.

He was more handsome than any photo could capture and she was only slightly ashamed that she'd imagined him sad about his breakup with Emma.

Abandoning that line of thinking, she focused her attention on the scenery once again. A few minutes later Lucas pulled into the parking lot of a home-improvement store. "Why does everyone have so much wood?" she asked, noticing sheets of plywood on all the trucks.

"We have a lot of windows to protect from the hurricane. I just need a few sheets. You game?"

"Sure. What else do I have to do?"

They got out, and her hair danced in the wind. A stray shopping cart, spurned on by the wind, headed for her. She caught it and pushed it toward the entrance without missing a beat.

Emma would have had a fit.

Lucas stopped that train of thought because Emma wouldn't have even been at the hardware store with him.

Doreen stopped just inside the door and he came up short, his hand landing on the small of her back.

"This isn't appropriate." Doreen turned around and seemed ready to leave.

He moved his hand although he didn't want to. "What?"

"We need one of those types of carts for the wood." Her look said she was confused. "Where's everybody getting those? Our buggy is wrong."

"Just leave this one," he told her. The wood he needed seemed to be leaving the store quickly, which meant they were in danger of running out. "We'll find one while we're inside."

When they entered the store, Doreen veered off toward the wallpaper department.

"You coming?" he asked.

"No, you go ahead. I think I'll look around. See what I can find."

Lucas hurried over to the lumber department, pulling on his gloves, just as another man reached the same section of wood. They split the remaining wood and Lucas loaded it onto a spare cart.

He bypassed the cutting area in search of Doreen.

There was no custom cutting on pre-storm days. Sheets were split in half, and that was it. If the line had been shorter, he'd have saved himself the trouble of opening his workshop and cutting the wood himself. But that would add an hour to his wait, and he didn't want to waste the time.

He grabbed a pack of blades and more gloves, and stopped himself from picking up more duct tape. Several rolls of it were somewhere at home. He just had to find it in the shamble of a workshop. Organization hadn't been a priority. Not with everyone hurrying to get the house done in time for Emma's arrival.

And now she wasn't ever going to come. The irony wasn't lost on Lucas.

Walking the top of each aisle, he looked for her and found Doreen a couple aisles down looking at flashlights, a basket on her arm.

Doreen acknowledged him with a smile and came toward him. Men turned and followed her movement as if she were on a runway.

Her clothing was completely wrong. The black short-waist jacket with the big metallic buttons hugged a chest that was curvaceous enough to make men glance first, then openly admire her. The fitted black pants complemented a figure that visited the gym and spinning class on a regular basis yet didn't say she was a gym rat. He hated "I have zero percent body fat" type people anyway, and Doreen wasn't one of them.

She'd once confided how much she loved working out. It calmed her down when she got tired of working with frustrating people. He couldn't help wondering what else helped calm her down.

Lucas wondered as to the direction of his thoughts, given that he'd just broken up with Emma. How could he be thinking about Doreen when he'd just ended things with his fiancée?

He slowed his cart as Doreen approached, and smiles fell off the faces of the men that she passed. When she stopped in front of him he almost expected lights to flash over his head like he'd won a jackpot.

Lucas looked into her basket, filled with safety glasses, sturdy work gloves, flashlights, gum, and a men's magazine on fitness that boasted an article on what men wanted. The top had an official seal on it and he regarded it closely. It was the word *official* that struck him.

The relationship with Emma had been over for a long time. They'd just made it official today. Lucas sighed, having come to the sound conclusion he'd known in his heart for a long time.

"You could have just asked," he said to Doreen, referring to her magazine. "I could have told you what men want."

Embarrassment crept over her face. "You're such a know-it-all."

He guided her away from two men who'd begun a heated argument over two remaining bags of sand and he steered Doreen into a slow-moving checkout line.

"You've got nails?" she asked.

"Yes."

"And you hammer them right into the house?" she asked, shifting from foot to foot in the long line.

Lucas nodded. "That's right."

"No boards to protect the frame or anything?"

The question sounded odd to him, but he didn't ask for clarification. "No."

"So every storm you put new holes in the house?"

Other people in line who could hear their conversation smiled at Lucas, but Doreen was oblivious as she flipped through her magazine.

"Yes, new holes. Every storm. Why?"

"Charging almost a million dollars for a tiny house with a bunch of holes in it that might get washed out to sea sounds like a rip-off to me. But nobody asked my opinion. You can't get away with that anywhere else, but this is Florida."

People around him chuckled.

"It's a beautiful place most of the time," a woman told Doreen. "Everybody understands about the holes. Besides, we don't have storms often."

Doreen seemed shocked that the woman was even talking to her.

Lucas wanted to laugh but didn't.

After that, she waited patiently until their turn approached. At the register, she rushed over to a basket that had just been delivered. Lucas immediately knew what she wanted.

"If you get caught in a hurricane, that rain slicker isn't going to help you," he told her.

"But they have pink. Do you want one?" she asked him.

"No."

"Not pink," she said over her shoulder. "Seafoam green. And it's my treat."

Amidst a store full of laughing customers, Lucas groaned.

Lucas was quiet all the way home, and Doreen guessed it was because of the ribbing he'd taken at the store. "I didn't mean to embarrass you back there."

"Forget about it."

So she *had* embarrassed him. She had to remind

herself that she wasn't in New York and she couldn't railroad a man just because she was accustomed to doing things her way.

This was his town and his home-improvement store and she was leaving in a day or two and the last thing she wanted was to cause him undue stress.

They rounded the corner on Waterwillow Street and a gray house came into view.

"Oh my. That's it. I imagined it a hundred times and it's just like I saw it in my head." Doreen looked at Lucas. "Your house is gorgeous."

"You recognize it?"

"Of course."

Although she couldn't decipher his expression, his mouth wasn't set in a hard line anymore like her uncle Angel's after her mother died and he had to care for her. She guessed he was probably still feeling the effects of his breakup with Emma, and she had to be cognizant of his feelings.

Her presence was a reminder of what he'd lost. She'd be here for only twenty-four hours, and she'd make sure he didn't regret inviting her to stay.

He pulled into the yard and she got out of the truck. "The heat is stifling."

"Gets real hot before the storm blows in. Very humid. You'll be perspiring until you get back on the plane."

"But there was a nice breeze when we were at the store."

"Didn't say there was a rhyme or reason to the storm."

Doreen couldn't take her eyes off the house. "It's just like you described it. Every detail."

"Wait until you see the inside."

He genuinely sounded like he wanted her to. She walked to the back of the truck and waited for him to lower the gate. "Do you need help with the wood?"

"No, I've got men to help me unload. You can go inside."

Mo walked out of the house and headed down the stairs. Doreen recognized him right away from Lucas's description and met him on the grass.

"You're not Emma," he said.

"Hi, Mo. I'm Doreen Gamble."

"Hey, Lucas, you found a very beautiful woman at the airport and brought her home," Mo called out in a teasing tone. "What did you do with the other one?"

"Nothing. She didn't come," Lucas told him, pulling the wood from the truck.

"But you found something better." He pulled Doreen in for a hug and talked over her head to Lucas. "She's real pretty."

"I hate to break up your lovefest, but could you help with the supplies?" Lucas sounded edgy as he pulled the wood down, one sheet at a time. Doreen reined in her happiness at Mo's welcome. At least someone liked her. Lucas suddenly seemed surly.

"I'm busy escorting my future wife," Mo told him, all smiles.

"You move quickly, don't you?" Lucas asked.

"When I see what I want, I go after it," Mo told her, gesturing as if the road was open ahead of them. "Not like some people who think about life as if it were peanut butter. Crunchy or smooth. Ten times back and forth. What is that about?" His lip curled. "I pick smooth every time."

"Okay, Mr. Smooth. What about Armella, your current wife?" Even Lucas couldn't help but smile at Mo's charm.

"Who?" Mo looked like he had no idea what Lucas was talking about.

Doreen gave Mo a look of suspicion. "I don't want to get you into any trouble."

"Trouble is my middle name, pretty lady. Don't you worry. I can handle anything that comes my way."

"Handle this wood," Lucas told him.

"Excuse me," Mo said to her. "He can't do a thing without me." He turned and whistled and two men came out of the house.

They greeted her with a nod.

Doreen couldn't contain her laughter. "I have something for you, but I want to help Lucas. It looks like it's going to rain again."

"It's the rainy season. You've got something for me?" Mo looked flattered as he rubbed his hands together. "That's right. Mo has talent he didn't even know he had."

The other men harassed him as they unloaded the truck and took the wood to the shed.

"Not just for you," Doreen told Mo. "For all of you."

She went to the two men and shook their hands. "Rog, Horatio, it's nice to meet you."

"How do you know my name?" Rog asked her.

"Lucas told me. We talk about the renovations every day, and he would tell me little things about you men and how hard you were working. The house is gorgeous."

The men smiled, and Doreen opened her red suitcase.

"My company gives away all kinds of promotional trinkets, so I set these aside for you guys. I was going to send them with Emma, but since she couldn't come, I brought them with me. Just as a thank-you for all your hard work. If it's okay with Lucas."

She turned to him and he played with his baseball cap, looking just as captivated as the guys. "Sure. What you got there?"

"I heard that Mo was the big boss around here."

Mo stuck his chest out, his white T-shirt flapping a little at the bottom. "You heard correct. I run this show."

"Every boss needs a hat." Doreen pulled from a special cloth bag a blue hat she'd had specially inscribed *El Presidente.*

Mo saw the hat and his eyes lit up. "How did you know? I *am* the president!"

Flicking the other one off his head, he sat the new one gingerly on his dark swirling curls and gave a profile pose from both sides to the men, who laughed at him.

"This is an important day," he told them. "You will all address me as Mr. President."

In their own languages they scoffed at him.

He smiled at Doreen. "Don't worry about them. We know the truth."

"You're right, Mr. President," she said, ignoring Lucas's eye roll. "I was also told you loved Celia Cruz." She gave him a black iPod. "This is for you."

He grabbed his chest. "It's Christmas in August. I'll enjoy it now, because Armella will not let me keep it."

Doreen gave him a pink one for her. "Now you both can have your own."

"Thank you, *senorita bonita*. This is so nice and un-expected. *Gracias*." He hugged her and swung her like she was a rag doll.

"You're welcome." Doreen turned her attention to the other men, who looked on anxiously. "Well, for Rog, I know you have two little girls. Twins, Lucas told me. I saw these Snow White and Cinderella umbrellas and I thought these would be perfect to go with these raincoats. And Lucas said you and your wife are Italian, and what Italians don't like Pavarotti?" She handed him a CD.

"Bella," he murmured, and kissed both her cheeks. "We love Luciano. *Grazie. Grazie.* When I make love to my wife, she will appreciate you because of this."

Doreen couldn't take her eyes off Rog. His declaration enthralled her. Her gaze slowly moved to Lucas who winked. "Oh. Okay, Rog," she whispered. "You're welcome."

"Enough!" Mo told Rog, breaking the spirit of the moment. "We're not making a sex tape here."

"You Americans are so afraid of passion and love-making. That's why you die of divorce."

"We die of heart disease," Mo told Rog.

"Because you have no one to make love to because you are divorced. *Grazie, bella.*" He walked off reading the back of his CD, the frilly umbrellas under his arm.

"You're welcome. And finally, for you, Horatio." She turned to the twenty-year-old, who was Mo's nephew. "I understand that you're in college and that you needed an internship. I thought I'd offer you the opportunity to come work for me in New York for six weeks after you finish your job here. The pay will be low, like twelve an hour, but if you're interested, it's yours. If not, I have an iPod and a Jay-Z DVD."

The quiet young man with the coal black hair had been grinning at his friend's behavior, but had stayed back. She read intelligence in his dark eyes, which were studying her, too.

Her words registered, because his mouth fell open and he jumped in the air. "An internship in New York for money. In an office and not in the sun, right?"

"Right."

He jumped up and ran up on the porch, ran back down to Doreen, picked her up and spun her around. She was laughing when her feet touched the ground again.

"I've got to call Mamma! That's the best offer ever. Wait. Mo, can I go? Wait. When does it start? Can I have the iPod, too?"

Doreen nodded.

He whooped at this. "I'm giving it to my little brother. I'm going to New York. Mo, help me go to New York."

Mo held up his hands. "We have to talk to my sister first. He's the first to go to college, and he'll be the first to go far away, but this is a good offer. You're a good woman, Doreen Gamble."

"I can speak to her if you like." Doreen remembered how people had helped her after her mother had died. This was her way of paying it forward.

"You've done enough, *senorita bonita*. I will help him from here." Mo turned to the group as his nephew looked on with adoring eyes. "All right, you two, thank this beautiful woman and get back to work."

The heartfelt gratitude was more than she expected.

As the two men went back to work, Mo took her hand in his. "I will say right now that Lucas loved the wrong woman."

Her cheeks felt hotter than the warm breeze. "You're embarrassing me," she told him.

"That's enough, Mo." Lucas hadn't said a word throughout the entire thing, but now he spoke up.

"I do not lie," Mo told her with a wink and a smile.

Doreen waited at the top of the stairs on the wide porch fitted with rockers that were stacked on top of one another.

Horatio came back out onto the porch. "Lucas, you need to see the news."

Doreen stepped into the foyer and knew Lucas had been holding out on her. A granite foyer floor lay beneath the plastic. This was the big surprise. They'd covered it with plastic because they were walking on it, but she went to the corner and pulled it back for a closer look.

It was a gorgeous black-and-gray-speckled floor that had been cut and fitted perfectly into the foyer. Every piece shone like glass and was sturdy enough to last for a hundred years or more. Doreen ran her hands over the surface, awed. Rog's craftsmanship was brilliant.

From inside, the news blared. "The Weather Service has issued a new timeline for the return of Hurricane Ana, the storm that is gaining strength in the Atlantic and heading for the coast again. She could now come ashore within the next twenty-four to forty-eight hours. If you haven't gotten supplies, now is the time to get them before you hunker down. This is Connie Alvarez reporting from News 2."

"Guys, I think we need to call it a day," Lucas told them.

"What about the windows?" Horatio asked, looking between the men, concern on his young face. "Those were the first ones blown out last time. I can stay and get them boarded. We haven't even cut the boards." He started for the door.

"I'll do them," Lucas told him, stopping the young man. "I need you to go home and board up your mother's house. If she needs anything else, call. I can run by the store and grab her medicine."

"Thanks, Lucas, but I got this. I can't wait to tell her about the internship. I'll get her medicine and use the boards from before. I bought three extra sheets of wood the last time and stored them in the back room."

Doreen could still feel Horatio's excitement, but he'd turned back into a responsible young man looking out for his mother. He would be the perfect intern for Regents.

"Let's wait to tell Marie about New York after the storm, Horatio," Mo said to his nephew. "Once she sees how well she can handle things with just her and Michael, she'll be able to see you going to New York alone knowing she'll be fine here."

"I'll get Michael to help me board up the house and get the groceries."

"Good thinking," Lucas told him. "Rog, you head

home and get things ready for your family. I'll see you next week. Here's your paychecks."

Doreen slipped into the powder room and closed the door so they wouldn't thank her again for the gifts. She could hear Rog fussing about not finishing the floor.

Soon it was quiet, and a knock shook the bathroom door. "You can come out now."

Doreen opened the door, feeling silly. "How'd you know I was hiding?"

His look said he knew a lot about women. "They thanked you again."

She felt as if she was scanning him, but she needed to know the truth. "Are you okay with me giving them gifts?"

"I can't do anything about it now."

"I know, but—"

Why were his eyelashes so long? And why did they shutter his eyes when she really wanted to know what he was thinking?

He'd moved away from the bathroom and was now between the dining room and kitchen. His hand rested on the door frame as if he didn't want her to pass, but she didn't have anywhere else to go.

They were so close, she had to look up into his face, and all she could think about was using her lips to suckle his bottom lip.

"Do you have any wine?"

He walked into the kitchen and went to a built-in drawer, pulled out a bottle, opened it and poured two glasses.

When she followed him in, Doreen couldn't believe

her eyes. The kitchen was right out of *Home Architecture Today* magazine. "This was the kitchen in the June issue."

Lucas put his finger to his lips to shush her. "I heard that she liked it so much I copied it. It was supposed to be a surprise." He touched his glass to hers and toasted her before going through another opening she realized was the great room because she'd chosen the wainscoting. In every room she saw her ideas and suggestions, and she wondered if he knew Emma had never given a single suggestion for any of the designs for the house.

Doreen lingered in the kitchen, admiring every nuance, including the ceiling-high pillars in the four corners and the beautiful floors. It was the perfect place and even had a station for a computer. As she walked through the great room she noticed lighting had been placed strategically for furniture and paintings, though the room was still bare.

She walked out the door leading to the deck and found Lucas out there sipping his glass of wine. The ocean stretched into the distance behind his house and she felt the grit of sand against her skin and the taste of salt on her tongue. Lucas didn't seem bothered by the elements or the angry sea that sent white water foaming against the shore.

The deck was as long as the back of the house, large enough to entertain a crowd comfortably.

Holes had been drilled in the floor of the seasoned wood, she guessed for the table umbrellas needed for protection from the relentless Florida sun. A pit had been built off the deck where the grill would sit.

Enclosed and on the side of the deck sat a hot tub with its own private entrance to the house.

"What are you thinking about?" she asked him, her head a little light. Food would have been a smart choice before drinking, but she hadn't done anything in the right order today.

"You brought everyone a present but me."

He wasn't angry or joking. There was this "no games" manner to Lucas that took some getting used to. The men in New York merely said they weren't into games, but this man truly wasn't.

"I didn't think it was right to give this to you in front of everyone else."

Doreen pulled the velvet bag from her pocket and put it in his hand.

He set his glass on the rail and slid his finger inside the soft material. Despite herself, her legs felt weak. He upended it into his palm and the elaborate platinum-and-diamond engagement ring fell into his palm.

He flipped it over one time then put it back into the bag, shoved it into his pocket and looked her straight in the eye. "Do I get anything else?"

Her mind went blank. A metallic taste slid along her jaw until it reached her tongue. "Um…what do you want? I have another iPod. I was going to keep it for myself, but if you want it—"

"Keep it. I've got one."

His eyes looked like smoldering coals and she wanted to take him back to the days when they joked and pretended to fight about wallpaper. "I don't know what you want, Lucas," she whispered.

"Your lips. I want your lips."

It took the space of a second for him to have her back against the deck railing, and another to find the perfect fit for his body against hers. The wind picked up, swirling between their necks, and she caught the scent of Usher's cologne, an aphrodisiac when blended with the magnificent crush she had on him. All of him felt good against her as he leaned in and claimed her mouth as if it were his to have.

Chapter 5

Lucas thought nothing could be sweeter than watermelon that sixth summer in Kingstree, South Carolina, on Great-Grandma Babe's porch, where he'd spat black seeds from between gapped teeth as sticky juice ran down his chin and landed in speckled dots in the dirt between his feet.

That was until he kissed Doreen. Her lips tasted better than watermelon, better than Godiva chocolate, better than his guilty dreams of her from last night.

Lucas slid his hands up Doreen's back to her neck, and she resisted and pushed on his chest.

"Stop. I'm not Emma." She walked into the house and the door closed with a decisive click.

Lucas shook the railing with all his might and looked up into the dark, embattled sky for answers.

Lightning sliced his view of heaven and struck something in the distance. Sparks ignited and thunder boomed.

The storm was returning and they would probably lose electricity. His thoughts careened.

Had he just become unengaged and kissed his former fiancée's—what? He knew they weren't good friends. But what was their relationship? Was he putting Doreen in a bad position? He knew they'd no longer be working together, but he didn't really know all the details of their personal relationship. They might see each other at the same coffee shop and that might cause some discomfort. He didn't need to be the cause of any hard feelings.

Because he couldn't explain to himself why he wanted to know Doreen so badly.

It was like something in him had come alive. He really didn't feel bad about him and Emma. That relationship had been over for so long, it was like a baseball game where only one team had showed up to play. The game had been forfeited. Now he'd found someone more interesting to pay attention to. But he'd come on too strong and he'd pushed Doreen away.

"I must be stupid. No, I'm horny and stupid. Doreen is gorgeous," he said to the clouds. "I'm gettin' this all wrong. Damn."

Rain drizzled on him and he looked to the left and saw that the deck wasn't yet wet. How could he have his own personal rain cloud?

"I deserve that," he said to the sky.

Grabbing the wineglasses, he went inside and

flipped on the TV in the kitchen, then realized a lightning strike had hit the TV station's tower.

Opting for the radio and WLCK, he waited to hear if his college buddy Terrence "Holy Terror" Jeffries was on. As he did so, he washed the glasses.

"Winds have increased to 55 miles per hour, and residents are encouraged to pull in plants and animals." That wasn't a good sign. They'd just had a short reprieve from a bad storm a few days ago, and it seemed as if Hurricane Ana was reviving herself. It had rained all day and the sea was foaming. The swells were at least six feet high and happening with the frequency of quickening contractions.

"Surfers are loving the waves, but Beach Patrol will soon be shutting down access to the water because all rescue personnel will need to be on alert in case of civilian emergencies. This is Dana Montgomery for WLCK News."

Lucas thought about Doreen and he knew he had to apologize before he did anything else.

He set the clean glass on the counter, walked upstairs and checked all the empty rooms, but he couldn't find her. His heart pounded at the idea that she might have called a taxi and left. He'd have heard her, he reasoned, taking the stairs down to the gleaming, granite foyer floor. Rog had done excellent work.

There was no place to go but the airport, but Doreen might have felt desperate enough not to stay. He hurried down the winding staircase and turned toward his bedroom and saw that his door was closed.

Knocking, he waited and didn't hear anything.

Turning the knob, he stuck his head inside the room and saw Doreen curled up in his chair with the blanket from the bed over her body, her face partially covered. He stepped in and noticed she was asleep.

Relief overtook him. He was glad she hadn't been so pissed off that she'd left. Quietly he closed the door and let her sleep. He'd apologize later. Right now, he had to get the wood cut and up on the windows.

Grabbing his heavy slicker—not the seafoam green one Doreen had bought—he headed out the back door to the workshop and was pelted with a reminder that the sea was again coming ashore.

Lucas called Stephen, who was back at the house, to check in. "What's going on?"

"You let your crew go early today?" Stephen asked, his police radio going off in the background.

"Yeah, they're gone. How's it going for you?"

"Lots of house alarms going off and people getting worried about not having evacuated earlier. Have you checked on your mom's house?"

"I checked on it yesterday. It's fine. Look, I've got a question about women. Wait, how's Mia?"

"As good as delicious champagne."

"What happened with the property that was her father's? Did you give it back to her?"

"Yes, Lucas. Well, we worked out a deal. She's going to buy it back."

Lucas laughed as he pinned the flaps back on the shed and started setting everything up to cut the wood.

"You're charging her for her father's land? You know you're going to hell. What a man you are." Lucas knew exactly what to say to get under Stephen's skin, but his friend seemed unflappable lately, and barely reachable since Mia James had blown into town. Lucas was a little concerned that he hadn't met Mia yet.

"I paid good money for that land, Lucas. Why am I defending myself to you, a man who hasn't seen his woman in thirty-two weeks?"

Rain swept through the yard ushered in with lots of wind. It bowed the palm trees and fluttered the shutters against the house.

"Has Terrence gone off the air yet? He's been on, what, fifteen days in a row?"

"You exaggerate more than he does. Do you know that?" Stephen asked, laughing. "I think it's been six days. He's got it bad for Sherri."

"No different than you and Mia."

"Bruh," Stephen said, "I can't argue that."

Lucas laughed. "I'd better get going. I have to get the wood up on my windows and I need to do Ms. Lucy's place, too." His neighbor was in the hospital with a broken hip.

"Your guys didn't get that done before they left?"

"No, we ran into some unexpected delays, but the foyer floor is done."

"Yeah, that's all Emma's ever been worried about. That unfinished foyer floor. Look, I've got to go. School's been called off, and we've got to make sure we've got enough blankets for it to be used as a shelter. Check in later."

"Yeah, I'll do that. I'll hit T at the radio station, too."

"Morales out," Stephen said, and disconnected.

Lucas affixed the blades to the saw and started cutting the wood. It didn't take long for the intermittent rain to become steady, but he stayed focused and cut all the wood, even what he needed for Ms. Lucy's house.

He'd peeled off the slicker and hung it up long ago, the humidity and enclosed space making him feel like he was in a sauna. Down to a T-shirt and jeans, he worked for the next two hours.

Lucas was throwing wood onto the cart to pull to the house when he saw a pink slicker coming toward him from across the yard.

Doreen didn't have her suitcase and she hadn't snuck out the front door. She walked in and didn't say anything to him.

Lucas used a towel to mop his face as she looked around his shop. Then her gaze met his. "I brought you something to eat and drink."

He turned down the radio. "I'm sorry."

From beneath her slicker, she pulled out his lunch cooler and opened it. He took a step forward and peeked inside. She'd made sandwiches from chicken he'd had in the refrigerator and had brought him a quart of Gatorade. In baggies, she'd put carrot slices and potato chips.

A smile worked its way around his mouth and he felt good all over. A woman hadn't done anything like this for him in years. He wanted to hold her again, but he knew that would be the wrong move.

"Did you eat?" he asked, wanting her to stay close.

She nodded.

He took the sandwich but didn't open the wrapping.

"Say you'll forgive me." Their gazes met and she looked away first. "I won't feel right eating, knowing that you're angry with me."

Her pink fingertips disappeared under her slicker. "Why did you kiss me?"

Under the harsh light of the overhanging lamps she looked moody, but her voice was cautious. Like his answer had the power to solve a multitude of questions. "I wanted to kiss you, Doreen. I know you're not Emma. You're different from her in a million ways. You came all this way to break up with me for her. You brought my crew gifts. You made me a sandwich. She'd have never done any of that. Or bought a pink slicker or even gone with me to the hardware store. You're you. I'm not confused, Doreen Elizabeth Gamble. I knew who I was kissing, and I want to know more about you."

Her lips quirked, although she didn't smile. "You remembered my whole name."

"Yes, I remember everything we've ever talked about."

He pulled a dusty stool from under the worktable and wiped it off for her. She walked over from the door and sat down, loosening her slicker from her head. "And you wanted to kiss me?"

"Yes."

"Because you're horny? I heard you from your room. I opened the doors from your upper deck and you were standing right below. I was going to take a taxi back to the airport, but I didn't want to be stranded there."

"I shouldn't have said that, but I'd never take advantage of you." Lucas didn't want her to be afraid of him.

He crossed to her, slowly taking her hand. He brought it to his lips and kissed it.

Her gaze softened. "It was only a kiss. You didn't rape me."

"I would never hurt you. I'm trying so hard not to kiss you right now."

She looked at his hands and back into his eyes. "This has never happened to me before, and I don't trust it."

"You're a beautiful woman. God, you're gorgeous."

"Lucas, it has nothing to do with looks and everything to do with how I've been treated. How I've treated myself," she said quietly.

He finally understood. "Doreen, I haven't had a sexual relationship with any other woman in the last eight months. My most intimate relationship without sex has been over the phone with you."

The look in her eyes changed from caution to reluctant interest. His stomach made an untimely growl and he answered by biting into his sandwich. It tasted like it was from a New York deli. "I haven't tasted a sandwich this good since I was in the city."

"You have everything in your refrigerator. You just need to put the ingredients together the right way."

As she spoke, she dug into the cans of nails on his workbench and lined up the nails by size on the table.

She looked like she'd washed her face and her lashes were free of makeup. Her eyes were gorgeous. Every time she looked up at him, the muscles in his thighs jumped. He moved a nail and she watched his hand and then looked at him.

Sure enough, his quadriceps jumped.

Hot damn.

"I don't know why you're one of those insecure women who's beautiful but doesn't know it."

Doreen held the nails in her hand for a few seconds. "I'm secure, but I get twisted around by men who say they want me, but a week from now can't find my number."

"I'm not like that."

"For the record, every man says that." The cloud of disbelief and doubt was back again and he knew that he'd have to deal with it, no matter the level of their relationship. She looked in the can and pulled out more nails and started sorting them. A lock of hair stuck to her face and she used her fingernail to guide it off.

"I'm not every man. I've been talking to you every day for the last eight months, and I think you know me better than that. I shouldn't be lumped in with the rest of the pack. You should give me a chance."

"Is that what you're asking?"

"Yes."

Her eyes were big, her mouth slightly open. "Tell me what you know already."

"Your favorite color is pink."

"Who doesn't know that? I look like a piece of bubblegum."

"Your mother died when you were eleven, and you went to live with your uncle Angel. You didn't think he liked you because he never smiled. That's why you wanted your kitchen to be yellow when you grew up. You thought yellow was the color of a smile."

"That's right." Doreen got up and stood by the

doorway, as if she couldn't decide whether she was going to stay.

"You wanted white cabinets in the kitchen." He gestured to the house. "I kept asking you if you knew how hard they were to keep clean. I told you an oak color would be better."

"You're right. That whole design is gorgeous. The day I saw it, I fell in love."

Lucas saw her expression, but more than that he felt the weight of her words in his body. He'd always wanted someone to feel that way about him. Namely his wife.

Rain slashed against the ground, but didn't gain in intensity. He began loading the boards onto a rolling cart.

"Did you paint your kitchen yellow?"

A wry twist to her brow told him she had. "It's really tiny in my brownstone, but I did. It's pretty." She gave him a look that told him she wanted to know what else he knew.

"You wanted to go to NYU because it was a highly respectable university, but you wanted to stay near your uncle in Oswego, New York. He made you go to NYU, but you never told me why."

"He said he wanted me to follow my dreams. I'd been offered a partial scholarship to Cornell, but Angel paid for me go to NYU because that was my first choice. I never understood Angel."

Lucas wiped the moisture from the saw blades and pulled out the power cords. "He didn't want you to feel indebted to him, and look at you. You followed your own path and now you're going to be director of special events."

She nodded, but Lucas didn't see pride or excitement for the position on her face. He realized then that she'd talked about getting the job, but she hadn't said anything about wanting it.

The light outside was nearly gone. "I've got to get the boards up." He walked to her side of the table. "But before I go—you never forgave me."

"I do, Lucas. I forgive you."

"I have another question."

She'd gotten up and was trying to push the cart. "What?"

"I want to get to know you better. Do you have a problem with that?"

A thousand responses flashed in her eyes, making him want to kiss the confusion away. But Doreen wasn't a conquest. She wasn't a goal to achieve and then to discard. She was a woman he wanted to know. More than he'd ever wanted to know anyone before.

"What was your first response?" he asked her. "Before everything else just flew through your head."

"That's not really fair. There are strings attached to everything."

"Not true. Forget Emma and forget why you came to be here, and just think about you and me. Now what do you think? What was your first thought?"

Rain clicked against the ground sounding like a hundred rattle drums.

"Yes," she finally said. "I'd like that."

He breathed easier, as if he'd been granted a stay from a terrible fate. "Good." Lucas took her hand and kissed the back of it again. "I hope you're not one of those types of women who start off by feeding her man and then stops."

Quick and sassy, her smile tantalized him. "As long as he feeds me back."

"Oh, hell, yeah. I excel there and in other things."

Thunder shook the ground and she took her hand back. "I'm sure you do. That's why I'm going to help you maintain your high level of excellence. I'm going to help you."

Doreen put both hands on the cart and pulled. It didn't budge.

"No you're not. Go in the house where you're safe."

"I'm helping, Lucas. You have a lot of windows and I'm strong. If you show me, I can be a really good worker."

"Maybe that's what you're accustomed to in New York—women having to help because men won't be men—but not here."

"So you're sexist, too. I can honestly say I don't like what I see."

"I'm a realist. If you get hurt and can't go home, how mad are you going to be at me?"

"It will be my fault for trying to help you save the house you built. But who will fault me for that? Give it up, Lucas. I'm still going to help you."

He saw the look of determination in Doreen's eyes and gave in. This wasn't worth going to the mat over. "You're getting your way this time because it isn't a matter of life and death, but one day you're going to have to do what I say without argument. Got it?"

"Yes."

"Then put your slicker on. If you're going to die, you're not going to drown, that's for damn sure."

"I'll probably drown. I already told you I can't swim."

He pulled on his slicker, too. "Lucky for you there's not much of a pool waiting for you on the porch. Let's go."

"Lucas, thank you."

When he saw the sincerity in her eyes, he grabbed the cart and pulled it across the yard, letting her think she was helping by pushing.

Chapter 6

Doreen could barely lift her fork, her arms hurt so badly, but she didn't complain. She was glad she'd put the roast and potatoes in the oven before going outside to give Lucas his sandwich, otherwise they'd have had cold food for dinner. After being out in the rain, the idea of another sandwich turned her stomach.

Earlier, she'd been hoping to go home, but now she was glad that she'd stayed. Lucas would have had to board up both houses alone, and even with two of them, it still took three hours.

Putting everything aside, she wanted to know Lucas personally, not through the veil of a professional relationship. And, to be honest, his kiss had opened a door she'd never thought she'd see the other side of.

The scent of strawberry caught her attention, and she realized her hair was still damp from her shower. Under normal circumstances no man would have seen her without her hair done and her face fully made up. But these weren't ordinary circumstances.

There was nothing pretentious about the fact that she was wearing Lucas's T-shirt and sweatpants, looking crazy in the head.

If she'd been home in New York, she'd have been thinking of ways to hide from him.

"You tired?" He looked so self-assured as he chewed his roast. "Arms hurt?"

"Not really." Her fork hit her plate and ketchup splattered onto her borrowed wife-beater T-shirt.

As Doreen wiped the shirt, she noticed his look. "What's the matter?" She looked at the mess then back at him.

"Those used to be my favorite shirts."

"Sorry. I'll buy you some more."

"Baby, they're my favorite again."

Innuendo seeped into her fatigued muscles and generated a tired smile. "You're hilarious. Do we have anything else to do tonight?"

It was pitch-black outside, and the rain sounded like hundreds of trick-or-treaters running around on the deck.

"We're done. We'll do the kitchen windows tomorrow. It looks like the Weather Service is right. Ana may come back by tomorrow."

"I won't be able to go home."

"I'm not sorry about that."

Truthfully, she wasn't so sorry, either. But she

didn't tell him that. "How long do hurricanes last?" she said instead.

"There's no real time frame."

"Days?"

"Could be. It's the aftermath that takes time. You know what happened with Katrina, but nine times out of ten it's not that bad. Again, I apologize about the travel situation and the fact that I have no furniture."

"Don't. You can't fly airplanes, and I know the furniture was supposed to be delivered this week."

Even though it was after midnight, Lucas looked sexy and not at all tired. Then again, he was the one who had decided to stop boarding the windows, not her. Probably because he valued his life, she amended. Her arms had been shaking pretty badly out there trying to hold the boards and the electric nail gun.

Her arms and chest muscles burned from exertion, and if she had to keep her eyes open another hour, Doreen thought she'd start to speak in tongues. She yawned, her hand over her mouth.

Lucas walked over to the kitchen windows and looked out as if he could see the ocean so far in the distance.

"I thought I'd planned everything so well, but it doesn't matter now. The highway's closed. There's bedroom furniture in my room and one room upstairs."

"Where am I sleeping?" Doreen stretched, and spun around on the stool.

He gazed at her from the window. "We could save the trouble of me dreaming about you and you could sleep with me."

The swell of sexual interest within her wanted to push common sense out to sea with the tide.

She'd had to run earlier, unsure if he knew that she wasn't Emma, but now that she knew that he knew, she was in serious danger of pouring all of herself at his feet. And she couldn't do that.

"You see, Lucas, in my old life, I would have accepted that offer thinking, 'He wants me forever.' The chemistry's there and we would have hit the sheets, and it would have been on until tomorrow."

"And now?" he asked, his gaze on her. She was glad they were having this talk. She could air her dirty laundry in advance and let him know even though she thought he was sexy as hell, he wasn't getting any.

"You've had a change of ideology," he said before she answered.

"Yep." She braced her hands on the counter.

"So when you said 'on until tomorrow,' did you mean it?"

He was tempting her with his subtle questions. "Why? That's all in the past."

"I want to know the type of woman you were versus who you are now. That's all."

She gauged his response. "That's right. My ego would have led me to believe that being on all night would have cemented a relationship. But I can't play myself like that anymore."

He walked over and the closer he got, the more her body was drawn to his. His arm grazed her hair and she caught the scent of the strawberry shampoo again.

"What would have happened the next day?" he

asked her, his voice low, husky. "You know…after you broke it off on me and I, according to you, didn't call you back?"

He freshened their wine, then she felt his hand graze her back before he went to sit on the bar stool. He put her glass at her seat so she had no choice but to go back and sit down.

As she joined him, she was aware that she wasn't wearing a bra beneath the thin T-shirt and that when he'd touched her back, her nipples had responded.

She sat down and sipped her wine, conscious of the slight distance between herself and Lucas, the buzz in her head and how much her words didn't match her feelings.

Lucas moved closer and she could feel him practically surround her as he breathed softly against her cheek. "You didn't answer my question."

"If you didn't call me back, feelings of insecurity would haunt me," she said quietly. "But I'd wait until the second day to text you. 'Hey, had a good time.' Or something like that." She shrugged her shoulder and moved a fraction of an inch away.

"No, don't run this time. Come back. You have to learn to trust me."

There were three things she knew immediately.

No man had ever said those words to her; he wasn't playing and her heart was beating really hard.

Lucas didn't move toward her but waited.

Doreen closed her eyes.

"Open your eyes," he said softly.

She opened them and moved back where she'd been. "Okay?" she asked.

"If that's as close as you want to be. I kind of like you right here," he said and got closer, where his long legs brushed hers and his arms were almost around her. "What would happen if I didn't answer your text?"

Doreen had nearly forgotten their conversation. "I'd think about everything we'd talked about. Had I been funny enough? Too funny? What happened? I'd sweat the whole situation, and I'd end up walking from work to the gym farthest from my job just so I could think and so I could get you out of my system."

"Damn, I'm sorry in advance," he said. Then, unexpectedly, he leaned over and licked her shoulder.

Shocked, she drew her arm away and burst out laughing. "What the hell was that?"

"That wasn't good?"

His feigned innocence only heightened his charm. "You're crazy." *And gorgeous.*

"It wasn't good if your shoulders are still up. Settle down. You've got goose bumps. That's so sexy. I gave you goose bumps."

"Lucas," she warned, leaning away, but he wouldn't let her go too far.

"I'd call," he reassured her.

Thunder rumbled in the distance.

He rested his chin on her shoulder, his forehead on her ear. "I'd make such crazy love to you, you wouldn't be able to walk to the gym. And I'd call you the next day."

He wrapped his arm around her waist, grabbed the chair and bit her shoulder.

Stunned, she put her hand on his thigh and braced herself as he ran his lips up her shoulder to her neck.

His tongue was warm, his lips firm, but not demanding enough to break her will.

She knew this by instinct, just as she knew he was hardening for her before her hand journeyed up his thigh to his sex.

The thin rubber band that bound her hair disintegrated in his hands and he made her look at him as she dragged her nails up his T-shirt. She reached his neck and touched his cheek.

"Okay. You'd call. I have to go to bed now. Alone."

His arm was still tight around her, his fingers in her hair.

"Come on." His voice sounded rough, like he'd been yelling at a football game, but he wasn't angry with her as he helped her up. "Let me show you where you'll be sleeping."

He took her purse and walked up the stairs. Doreen didn't miss the fact that Lucas's hand stayed on the small of her back.

"There are two bedrooms down here," he said, referring to the left side of the hallway that was shaped into a U. "This is a walk-in linen closet."

"We don't have these in the city." She looked inside at the room with its shelves full of pastel and striped linen.

There were thick comforters and blankets neatly folded on one side, making her think of how much fun it would be to undo all the blankets and make love on them.

"Are you sleepwalking?" he asked, looking down at her.

"I wish I had one of these at home. I bought a bed

with drawers built into the bottom. That's where I keep my linen."

"Space costs here, too; it's just thought of differently. Here, it's a luxury. The first bedroom is empty, but the second one has pretty white furniture from Cohen and Stone. I didn't get all the curtains up, but the bed is made. The bathroom is through here." He set her purse on the dresser and flipped the bathroom light on.

Even with her bones feeling as if they were weighed down by boulders, Doreen didn't miss a detail. She remembered describing this room to Lucas, the tall, four-poster king-size bed, the sleep-comfort mattress, and the dressers with matching round tables.

He'd even remembered the thick bamboo area rugs that were on each side of the bed. This was the perfect guest room.

"It's beautiful. I can't wait to sleep in here. But I'm afraid I won't enjoy it, I'm so tired."

"You will. If you need anything, you know where to find me. Good night, Doreen."

"Lucas?"

"Yeah," he said, already at the door.

"I need some pajamas."

He seemed at a loss for words. "I sleep in boxers, baby, and Emma brought night clothes with her. The best I can do is give you another T-shirt, if I have one. My clothes aren't all clean. I got a little behind. Or you can sleep in that one."

She looked down at the ketchup she'd spilled on it. "I guess I can try to wash it off. You know what, never mind. I'll be asleep by the time you get back." She couldn't stifle a yawn.

Lucas watched her, smiling, then peeled off his T-shirt. "This is clean. I just put it on."

She took the shirt, her mouth hanging open. Nothing but muscle and man. "Oh, my God. Please go away."

He started laughing. "Sweet dreams, baby."

"Yeah, thank you."

Doreen pulled off her clothes and brushed her teeth with the brand new toothbrush that was on the sink before dragging the T-shirt over her head.

She'd made it. Lucas and Emma weren't anymore. She'd made it through the day without compromising herself, and now she was going to get a good night's sleep before heading home tomorrow.

Overall, she'd done well, even if kissing Lucas had sent her into an alternate universe.

Tomorrow, she had to leave this island.

Climbing into the center of the bed, she felt drugged yet surrounded by Lucas as she sank under the comforter and fell into a deep, restful sleep.

Chapter 7

A rhythmic sound bumped him from his dreams and wasn't like any storm he'd ever heard before.

It was synchronized.

Lucas pushed up on his elbows, his eyes still closed, his sex hard, the erotic dream he'd been having of him and Doreen too hot to want to escape.

Her breathing was fast, her body yearning. His fingers were in her as she arched into him, her arms bringing him close. He couldn't get enough of her as her long legs slid down his, capturing his sex at their apex.

He pulled himself too hard and his eyes popped open. "Ow, damn."

Lucas looked around his bedroom and saw that he was alone and the thumping continued. Daylight peeked through the shades, letting him know it was time to get up, but it appeared Doreen had risen early and was doing something to his house that had never been done before.

He got out of bed and his sex protested. He'd have to piss this one away.

Cleaning himself up took a little longer, but he was curious to find out what she was up to.

Walking from his room, he smelled food. And not fast-food-type junk, either. Real home-cooked food. He got to the kitchen and there were pots on every eye on the stove, bubbling at sufficient levels. His stomach growled in happiness.

Barked instructions came from the great room, where Doreen was in the most interesting outfit he'd ever seen.

Her bra, his sweatpants and a pair of his old work boots. Her back was to him as she worked out to a TV boot-camp program.

The instructor commanded they squat, and she did.

Her ass was phenomenal. All he wanted to do was climb into his sweatpants and *be* the pants.

The drill sergeant commanded they run in place and she ran with her legs wide, and when the man said drop and do twenty push-ups, Doreen dropped and did twenty.

Lucas watched her arms and back and listened to her exhale as she extended into each push. She was impressive, to say the least.

He must have made a noise because she recoiled and turned.

"My goodness, Lucas. You scared me. How long have you been standing there?"

"I don't know."

"You don't know?" She grabbed a washcloth and covered her breasts.

"This isn't the Garden of Eden. I've seen breasts before," he told her.

"You've never seen these before. I hope I didn't wake you."

"You did, but it was time for me to get up. Catch your breath before you pass out," he suggested. What he wouldn't give to save her. "Coffee?"

She stood and grabbed a glass of ice water that had been on the counter. "I've got to cool off a bit first. Do you work out?"

"Yep. Every time I climb up on the roof. That's my pull-ups. Stacking bricks covers my weight lifting. I do my best running when lightning strikes."

She was still breathless and that suited her. "I don't do anything as physical so I have to work out or I'd have a big, fat butt."

He rather liked what he'd seen in all her poses. "There are a lot of men who appreciate a woman with a healthy one. They have their place in the world."

"Not on this train," she said with a smile. "I've got to cool down and get cleaned up, then we can get to work. Oh."

"What?"

She hooked the washcloth in the front of her bra again. The effort was self-defeating. All it did was make him focus even more on her cleavage. She started stretching with her arms over her head, leaning to one side then the other.

"I need to go to the store," she said, inhaling then

exhaling slowly. "A store where I can get personal things; tennis shoes, pants and tops."

"My boots not working too well?"

She glanced at him, then kicked off his boots and peeled sock after sock. She went back to the center of the floor and stuck her foot out behind her in some type of yoga pose.

Her chest rose and fell, her arms straight as arrows. None of this was for enticement, but he wanted to lay her down spread-eagle so he could have fun with her.

"I used four pairs of your socks to make the boots fit."

He didn't believe her. "You came into my room?"

"I really needed to work off some of the stress, so I knocked and when you didn't answer, I tiptoed in and borrowed the pants, socks and boots from your closet. I hope you're not angry."

She changed positions and did something where her foot was stuck to her inner thigh and her hands were in the prayer position over her head. As she slowly brought her hands down, the washcloth fluttered to the floor.

For a man who hadn't made love in eight months, Lucas complimented himself on his self-control, but he couldn't stop himself from admiring every inch of her exposed flesh.

Doreen had beautiful smooth skin, and she was sexy, but it was her confidence to stand before him and not care that made him want to have her.

She'd pulled her hair back and braided it, but the end was coming undone.

If she only knew how turned on he was at her stretching, she would stop.

"I didn't mean to invade your privacy. I was in and out in five seconds."

"I'm not angry." Lucas made his coffee and turned on the TV in the kitchen. The low reception gave him a clue as to the weather's condition. He eyed the pots of food cooking on the stove. "If I'd known you were in my room, you'd have never gotten out of there. Do you know you have the most perfect belly button I've ever seen?"

"Thank you. My mother put a silver dollar on it to keep in. I suppose that was the thing to do back then." She stuck her finger in the little hole and all he could imagine doing was enjoying kissing it while making love to her, but he kept the thought to himself.

Doreen then came into the kitchen. Her black bra was cutting low between her breasts. She used the cloth to blot her temple.

"Where'd your T-shirt go?"

"It got superhot and I didn't know how to turn the air on—and, yes, I tried. I started getting a heat rash so I figured I'd let my body air out a little. I put my T-shirt and the rest of my clothes in the washing machine."

"Heat rash? I thought only little kids got that."

"Yeah, just like only little kids get chicken pox," she replied sweetly.

"You're so charming your fangs almost don't hurt."

"Look at my arms." She walked over and showed him her inner forearm. "And my back."

There were splotches of red bumps clustered on her arms and back and her stomach.

"I see them, but I can't help but look at your perfect neck and lips and collarbone."

She grabbed her washcloth and, with an arched brow, hooked the cloth inside her bra. The trick was effective, but everything else was still exposed. "You might need a burkha to get me to stop looking at you. Now that you're this close, and now that I've touched you, I don't want to stop."

"You're really cute," she told him with a sweet sarcasm he found attractive. "I had the same reaction to you last night. I think we're both a little deprived."

"So we should go to bed and make each other feel good."

Thunder rumbled and rain slashed the deck.

"Life isn't always about feeling good," she reminded him.

Doreen looked out the kitchen window and sighed before going to the stove. The sexy banter ended as static blared out of the TV.

"I guess we should feel lucky we had any TV at all. The station was hit last night by lightning."

"How do you know?"

"I saw the strike. We need to get a move on, but I'll check on the air conditioner before we go in case I need to pick up a part. You should have a top on. Any of the men could show up."

"On a Saturday?"

"Well, no."

"If you're uncomfortable, I'll shower and change into more of your clothes right now."

"You could be naked right now and I'd be very happy."

"You are a man of contradictions. First you tell me to cover up, and now you'd be happy if I was naked. Which is it?"

"If I could have my way, I'd choose the latter, but since you have challenges, you can slide by." He smiled at her and watched her busy herself with the pots on the stove.

"I'm not trying to take over your house. I promise," she said, looking inside the stove.

Lucas had never seen anyone more determined to do for him. He and Doreen talked every day, and she'd never told him how domestic she was.

"Did you cook for Angel?" He slid onto a bar stool and watched her.

She nodded. "He was really smart, but he was a terrible cook, so when I moved in I just took over his kitchen. He never once complained. Before I finally left for college I cooked ten meals for him. He died on the eleventh day." She smiled at Lucas. "What a cool thing to do."

If he'd been a crying man, he'd have broken down. "You're something special, you know that?"

"Angel always said I was."

"Did you believe him?"

She nodded hesitantly at first then more decisively.

"I cooked all this food because Holy Terror said everyone lost power during a hurricane last year and didn't get it back for days. Your refrigerator was full and you're so busy, I thought I'd help you. All your food would go bad and then what would you eat?"

"I never thought of that. That happened once before, and I had to replace about four hundred dollars' worth of meat between my mom's house and mine. I usually keep less than fifty dollars' worth of food here now."

"Well, if it's cooked, you can enjoy it for a day or two before having to toss it all in the garbage." Her gaze sought his only to return quickly to the boiling pot of soup.

"Were you all alone after Angel died?"

"I don't have any more blood relatives, but I have some very best friends, so no, I wasn't alone."

"In all the times we talked you never mentioned them."

"It wouldn't have been appropriate."

He shrugged. "I want to know now," he said, loving how she puttered in his kitchen. Her feet made slapping sounds across the floor, and he made a mental note to buy her some slippers and a pack of her own T-shirts while they were out.

"Who are your best friends?"

"I have three. Pinky, Alicia and Cynthia. I've got more friends, but these girls and I go back to high school, and they remember my mother and Angel."

"They know all about you."

"That's right. Who knows you?"

"Terrence and Stephen. I went to college with those boys. They were with me when my father died, when my mother had her first heart attack and they still call to harass me. They're like women."

She wiped down the counter and cabinets when she finished stirring the pots and he got the impression she was just trying to keep busy. "You don't want them checking on you?" she asked.

"I'm fine. In fact, I talked to Stephen, and he said I was being honored for saving my neighbor's life. Ms. Lucy fell and broke her hip, and the mailman and I got to her and stayed with her until the paramedics arrived."

"Wow, Lucas. That's so amazing. When's the honor?"

He shrugged. "I don't know. I'd prefer they didn't do anything. I feel bad for not having checked on her earlier."

"Don't minimize it. You saved her life. That's pretty awesome." Doreen touched his hand. "I like you for it."

Lucas puffed up his chest. "Well, then I don't mind the attention." He went over and looked out the window before coming back.

"Didn't you say your father's family lived in the city?"

He nodded. "Harlem. I used to go up there every summer and stay with Uncle Dewitt and Aunt Helen. They didn't have any children, so it was a bit strange being with them."

"How'd you like it?"

He shook his head. "I hated it at first. Leaving my friends, and the ocean, and my toys. Please, I used to cry like crazy."

Doreen clapped, laughing. "Did your father care?"

"Hell, no. We would drive the whole way, too. That's when sleeping at rest stops was okay. My mom would hand me bologna sandwiches over the seat and tell me not to get crumbs on the seat. How could I?"

Doreen threw up her hands. "You were surrounded by luggage?"

"Right!"

They burst out laughing. "They didn't have any respect for you."

"No, they sure didn't," he said. "I miss that man." Lucas thought lovingly about his father. "Dad was soft-spoken and never raised a hand to me. All he had to say was, 'Lucas, I'm disappointed in you.'" Lucas grabbed his chest and looked into Doreen's eyes. "My heart would break. 'Daddy,'" he imitated, pretending to cry as his knees got weak, "'I'm sorry.'"

"Aww," Doreen said, putting on a sad face as she stifled a laugh. "They had you going. It should have been the other way around."

Lucas stood up and frowned, thinking. "You know…" He pounded the counter with his fist. "Now that I think about it, I used to hear laughing in their room after one of his two-minute talks. They were laughing at me?"

Doreen didn't hold back her laughter. "You're just catching on? Yeah, they got you good."

"I can't say that I like your attitude much either, young lady," he said, giving in to his own fit of laughter at his parents' duplicity.

"Oh, you've lost all your cool points with me. I'm disappointed in you," she said, and burst out laughing again. "I'm sorry, Lucas. I'm glad he wasn't cracking you over the head," she said, watching the pots. "Did you come to like the city?"

"I did. Uncle Dewitt was cool, and he taught me independence. I learned how to ride the subway and take trains and buses, manage my money and walk. Down here you have to drive everywhere except to the beach. My mother wasn't letting me walk to the store like in the city."

Doreen grinned. "My grandmother in North Carolina used to make me go outside all day. I had no idea what to do. I used to sit on the stairs and look at the dirt."

"The ants didn't eat you up, didn't they?" he asked, laughing.

She showed him her ankles. "Look. I still have the scars after all these years. My mother was furious, but that was her mother and she wasn't about to tell Granny she was wrong for sending me outside all day. I learned how to shell beans, pick cotton, apples and watermelon, and to tell stories. I learned how to ride a bike. Did you?"

Lucas threw his hands up. "In my own defense, I lived in New York in the summers and we have cars down here, and the only people you see on bikes are tourists."

"So that's a no?"

"You're a fake city girl, Dorie."

Her stomach shook. "So you want to resort to name calling 'cause you can't ride a bike? Pathetic, Lucas. Really sad."

"For your information, I learned how to ride when I was thirteen."

Doreen squeezed her eyes shut. "Wait. Weren't you like ten feet tall?" She sounded like a real New Yorker, too, and he loved it. "Did you have a helmet and training wheels?" She held on to the counter to laugh.

Lucas laughed, too. "Look who's talking, Ms. Scared-of-the-rain."

"Not rain. More like thunder, lightning and hurricanes," she said, and rolled her eyes at him. She didn't know how much fun he was having. "So now it's just you and Terrence and Stephen?"

"And my mom."

"Where is she?" Doreen stirred the pots and reached into a cabinet for spices. She seemed to know exactly where they were. This was her kitchen, after all. Well, she'd brought the design to his attention during their first conversation, and he'd fallen in love with it. It wasn't the exact model from the magazine, but it was so close one would be hard-pressed to tell the difference. He'd thought this sleek style would please Emma with all the contemporary functioning and modern sophistication, but she'd never gotten a chance to see the kitchen, and now he was glad.

This was his house. And it was up to him to make it a home.

And Doreen had this way of looking at him that made him think she could see right through him.

"My mother is in Cairo. She has a traveling buddy, and she and her girlfriend plan a couple trips a year and do their thing."

"That's awesome. What about you. Do you vacation?"

A look of confusion crossed his face then slid into a smile of whimsy. "Maybe I'll find the time."

Quiet filled the space between them. The memory of their laughter dissolved what had been discomfort. "Can I ask you something, Lucas?"

"This sounds serious."

"It is, sort of."

He sat down. "Sure."

"What do you do when you feel like it's just you?"

"I looked for my soul mate."

"I see," she said.

"What did you do?" he asked.

"Nothing. I have great friends. I joined a foundation that helps young adults with grief. Now I'm an on-call counselor once a month. Well, when I'm home."

"You do that a lot. Help, I mean."

"I do?" She blushed and he watched color spread across her cheeks, and she resumed her wiping.

He got up and walked around the counter to see what she'd do. She moved to the other side of the counter and wiped over there. "You help young people. You helped me. Right before the rain almost washed you and your pink slicker out to sea. What do you do to help you?"

Doreen accidentally bumped him when she passed to turn off the rice and smothered pork chops. "It's not that I don't believe in soul mates. I just feel that they aren't realistic."

"That's cynical."

"Not really. Who can say that there's someone for everyone? Why do some people get married eight times? Is that fair to everyone else?"

"You're introducing variables that aren't realistic. In this house there are two people. You and me. There's a high possibility that I'm attracted to you. In fact, I *am* attracted to you. The question is, are you attracted to me?"

"Yes. But Lucas, New York didn't move any closer to Florida the last time I checked."

"We just crossed a bridge, Doreen. We don't have to burn it down. I'm just glad to know it. We'd better get our day started." Lucas pulled eggs from the refrigerator and a bowl from the cabinet. Doreen cracked the eggs and beat them furiously in the bowl.

He poured milk into the bowl and sat back down.

"I hope you'll let me know if you need my help over at Ms. Lucy's house with the windows," Doreen told him.

Lucas laughed as she scrambled the eggs.

"No, thank you. After you dropped my electric nail gun, then nearly electrocuted me, I'm not using you as my assistant anymore. I'll call Mo or Stephen."

"You're such a baby, Lucas McCoy. It was just a little shock," she said softly. "Anyway, I helped you and that's what counts."

"Do you always help so much?"

"Men, you mean?"

"I meant everyone, but we can start with men."

Her brows crinkled as she cooked the eggs. "I used to, but not anymore."

"Why?"

"People take advantage of you and take your kindness for weakness, and weak is one thing I'm not. I don't have a father, mother or uncle. How can I be weak?"

"You're right. You're not. Someone would be making a terrible mistake to think otherwise."

"I help because it's the right thing to do. People helped me along my path in life, so I help others."

Lucas didn't speak for a few seconds. "That would be a big mistake to underestimate you."

"Eat," she told him, as she put the scrambled eggs in front of him.

"Just eggs?"

"You're demanding, too? You're going to be one of those old men in your wheelchair, strapped to the pole at the nursing home and nobody comes to visit you because you complain too much."

He coughed, eggs in his throat, as he tried not to laugh.

She went to the stove and put on an oven mitt.

"My kids are going to visit me. You'll see." He smirked at the image she'd painted of him, it was so far-fetched. He'd always imagined a full house of family, even though he didn't have any now. "I'm having at least five kids and they'll have kids and they'll have kids."

"What kids?" she sassed. "You won't make any. You're so fussy nobody will want to get down with you."

Even as she said the words, he couldn't stop himself from watching her round behind. He knew he'd have fun convincing her.

"Where's my food, woman? I'm not arguing with you all day."

Her hand was on her hip and she was smiling at him. "See what I mean? Fussy." With that, she pulled a pan from the oven and served him steak with pearl onions.

"Where'd those onions come from?"

"A bag in the refrigerator. It said 'from Ms. Lucy.'"

Lucas smacked his forehead. "I forgot. The onions *are* from her, and I need to check the back door on her house and make sure it's locked."

"See? Memory is the first thing to go. Old dude."

She smiled sweetly as she gave herself a small piece of steak and put the rest on the stove.

He remembered his state this morning, his reaction to her working with him, and how he felt right now that she'd cooked for him in her bra and his sweatpants. He could easily forego food and make love to her all day.

"I've got your old dude right here."

Her stare was cocky. "I know you do. So what you gonna do about it?"

He didn't give her time to take off her oven mitts. Lucas was out of his seat in a flash, and she screamed and took off down the hall.

Chapter 8

"I'm sorry." Doreen couldn't stop herself from laughing, standing behind his bedroom door, the place she'd wound up in their playful game of chase. "I was just talking junk."

"I noticed. With your fancy oven mitts on."

She huddled behind the door, the mitts over her face.

"Okay, Ms. Trash-Talkin' City Girl. What else do you have to say for yourself? By the way, hiding behind your hands only works if you're three."

Doreen put her hands down and gave her captor her most innocent face. "I was just flirting a little. No harm done."

"Really? You didn't see how I woke up this morning."

"Tell me."

"You want to know?"

The idea that she was on his mind made her feel like a superhero, albeit in an unattractive outfit.

They had been at a crossroads, the place where his relationship with Emma ended at the airport. But now this road was new. "I'm sorry. I won't tease you anymore." The words were completely untrue. That had been her initial purpose. To flirt, have fun and not get too serious. If she kept their relationship in that realm, she'd go home happy and mentally healthy. Knowing she'd made him wake up hot for her emboldened her feminine ego, and she felt empowered and confident. This was the power of the "puddy," as Jay-Z and R. Kelly said in their song. She hadn't even used that aspect of her sexuality, and Lucas wanted her. But she had to be careful. Lust was an emotion that clouded reason, and sometimes she had to set the pace, or at least control it.

Doreen managed to squeeze past him and make it to the hallway before he caught her by the wrist and slowly took her hand. She liked that. A lot. "Where you going?"

"To the kitchen. I don't want the food to burn. Holy Terror said we should make ice, too. You have ice trays and an ice maker. Kind of strange to have both, but it works to your advantage."

This was neutral territory, talking about the storm, focusing on mundane topics that kept things in the realm of general interest. But his fingers against her palms made her imagine what they'd feel like all over her body. He was walking beside her, but she could just as easily see herself lying beside him—like this morning, when she'd tiptoed into his room and seen him twisted in his sheets.

The room had been as dark as the hallway was now. The air of intimacy was even greater now.

"There's still the matter of personal injury to me."

She fought a losing battle with a smile. She knew he wanted to kiss her so badly. And she felt the same. "And you're seeking restitution?"

"Not monetary. A kiss should square things between us. Of course, I'm asking first."

There was her old friend temptation again. Doreen reluctantly shook her head.

"Damn. Why?" Lucas sounded like he was this close to getting his way and she loved him for not getting a real attitude with her for turning him down. She wanted to laugh at his injured expression. He just didn't know that she was right there with him.

She quickly made her way to the kitchen, picked up the long fork and started moving the pork chops around in the pan. Then she stirred the beans in the other pot. She had to keep busy or she'd be on the floor, butt naked, having orgasms in every room.

"Lucas, I can't kiss you because…I have to brush my teeth."

He leaned on the counter, inches from her. "Let me be the judge of that."

He was fast, too fast for her to stop him from burying his face in her neck. Doreen burst into giggles and she couldn't contain her moans. "I'm dripping gravy all over the floor. Lucas! Stop it, I'm dripping."

"That's so erotic, baby. Say it again." He held her

hands out in front of her and hugged her waist. "If you'd behave and let me have my way with you, you'd be dripping in the very best way."

"I thought we had to get to the store." She said this even as she tipped her head to the side, granting him greater access.

"I'm trying to see something." He sniffed up her neck, around her ear, up her jaw, moving slower to her mouth. "You're right, your breath is terrible." He playfully smacked her on the hip.

A big laugh built and Doreen couldn't help herself. "You are so ridiculous." She turned off the stove and fanned the pots, then gave up pretending and fanned herself. "Holy Terror said we should have lots of ice. We need more Ziploc plastic bags." She dumped the tray of ice into a bowl, filled it and put everything back into the freezer. Grabbing the shopping list she'd started early this morning she added *bags* to her list.

"Did T call? I've told him about calling here at all times of the day and night. He doesn't sleep. The boy is crazy."

"No, he didn't call. I heard him on the radio. I think they were playing clips of a previous show, otherwise the man really doesn't sleep because he was on last night *and* this morning. He's got a great voice, and he and Sherri are so cute. I can tell he drives her crazy."

"He's totally into her and won't admit it."

"You said you went to college together, and now?"

"I can't shake the brotha."

She smiled at him. "You don't want to."

Lucas shook his head. "Him *or* Stephen. But

enough about those clowns. I've got to call them later today. Stephen's got a new house, and I just want to check that everything's going okay over there. And Terrence has been on the radio almost nonstop because of Hurricane Ana, so I think he's ready to fall over."

She couldn't help but think how nice he was. "His advice is good, considering I'm not from here and I have no idea what to do in a hurricane. He said go to a closet and keep a bag of clothes for each person inside. Take a video of your property. Get some extra money out the bank. Lucas, do you have photos of everything?"

"Didn't I tell you not to worry? Your forehead's all creased up and you're getting stressed out."

"I'm not." She wiped her eyes, completely comfortable with her body and him. "It's scary watching typhoons and hurricanes and floods on TV. You realize that nature can kill you. That's when you realize your own mortality."

"You're going to have to trust me. You're safe with me."

She regarded him quietly. "Okay, Lucas. But if I get lucky, the hurricane will hit after I'm gone. Or not at all."

The words sounded selfish, she realized, and she wanted to backtrack, but before she could he said, "That would be very lucky."

Doreen let the moment pass and poured green tea from a boiling pot into a pitcher.

"Where'd that come from?"

"My purse. I always have a couple bags with me. I'll pick up a box today. I can take it home when I go," she said softly. Closing the lid on the pitcher she shook the mixture until it foamed, then poured it over ice in a glass. Then she inserted a straw and held it out to him.

"No, thanks," he said. "I like my tea a dirty brown color and spiked with vodka, tequila, rum and gin."

"A Long Island Iced Tea. Ha, ha. This is good. Do you like sweet drinks?"

"Sometimes," he said, though he resisted her overture.

"Try it, please? I promise you'll like it."

"If I don't?"

"You can kiss me."

The words were out of her mouth before she could bite them back. Doreen wanted to kick herself. They'd so easily deflected their earlier intimate moment, and now they were going to be back into it because of her raging libido. She'd have to follow through this time.

She gave him her glass and watched him sip from it. "Do you like it?"

"Disgusting." Lucas set aside the glass and guided her to the bar stool, where he lifted her onto the seat.

"You're kidding. Are you lying to me?" she asked him, her body humming.

"No."

"It's just a kiss," she reminded him as he took her hand.

"Woman, don't tell me how to do my job."

She giggled a little. "I'm not, but gracious, how serious could this be?" She rolled her eyes.

"Shh," he told her, and she realized he was very serious.

His movements became deliberate as he leaned her

back and spread her arms wide on the granite counter-top. He touched the small of her back, and she automatically arched toward him, her eyes fluttering closed.

"Open your eyes," he whispered, his nose grazing her neck. He stayed close as if they were slow dancing, and his well-developed muscles and her sensitive skin were no match.

She was hyperaware every time they touched. The caress of his cheek against hers, his jaw on her shoulder, his nose on her elbow. Feeling him entice her was as beautiful as watching, which she'd never done before. Everywhere their bodies connected aroused her until she felt as if she were a pot, simmering.

Lucas blew on her stomach, and her muscles contracted as if they were reaching for him. Her heartbeat hammered, her lips parted, her breathing quickened in anticipation… But Lucas surprised her by going to his knees, his left hand on her right knee, his right hand on her left. Still no kiss, making her wonder just how long he was going to torture her.

He spread her legs wide, bringing her to the edge of the bar stool, the sweatpants pulling tight across her center, causing pressure to build on the inside of her thigh all the way to her navel. He blew again.

Doreen realized now that she had no idea where he was going to kiss her, and she had no way of stopping him from kissing her wherever the hell he pleased.

What she did know was that Lucas would soon know her secret. She was so hot for him, if he touched her anywhere south of her waist, she would climb onto his mouth and scream so loud the ocean would reverse course and the riches of sunken ships would be found buried on the ocean floor.

She thought then about knowing him and really *knowing him,* but as his tongue met her navel, all rational thought fled. He attacked her navel as if it was a rare delicacy, and though he didn't go lower, her butt left the stool, wanting him to. *Too soon, too soon,* warned an inner voice, and she accepted the pleasure she got with each lick and suck.

His strong hands anchored then released her, and without knowing when or how, he had her laid out against the counter. His strong arm braced her back while his mouth claimed her neck and clavicle and his hand roamed through her hair, caressing her face, neck, shoulders and stomach.

Never before did she want to climax so badly. At that moment she felt herself fall a little bit in love with him.

He wouldn't kiss her until she said it was okay. His hand continued its journey up her back and she caught it. "Sit down," she pleaded. She needed to put them both out of their misery.

He sat, his back against the counter, bringing her onto his lap, facing him, his hands riding her hips.

She wet her bottom lip, and his hand was up her back bringing their mouths together in an instant. His desire was as great as hers, she could feel it, but he surprised her with a controlled kiss. Then their mouths parted and like a dam bursting, his passion burst forth. His powerful thighs rocked her, their bodies simulating the intimate act. If this unconsummated movement were any indication, she could only guess the great depths of his virility.

She could go on kissing him for a lifetime, but when he buried his face in her bra and sighed like he'd just gotten home from a long day at work, she pulled away and brushed her lips against his cheek, her thumbs playing with the crisscrossed hairs on his unshaven jaw, her index fingers caressing his earlobes.

Yet it was her lips he sought again, raising her level of passion so high she thought she would come if he touched her navel just one more time.

She didn't get the chance, because something crashed against the house and they both jumped.

His lashes fluttered against her breasts and he gripped her hips just a bit tighter. "I need to see about that," Lucas said.

"I know." Doreen licked her lips and breathed deeply. She slid off his lap and brushed her wild hair from her face and mentally put a flat iron on her shopping list.

"Be careful." She offered the belated warning after he'd already struggled to stand and was looking out the kitchen window. "It might be an alligator trying to come inside. I heard that's a common occurrence down here."

He came back and cupped her face. "I'd still call the next day." His lips touched hers before he went to the back deck door.

A flash of desire shook her. Looking at her feet, she noticed her toes were even curled up. He was changing everything about her. She reached around to make sure her bra was fastened.

"Lucas, do you want me to look outside? You're still…out there." She gestured to his erection. "If it's a person, they'll know what we've been up to."

His look was one of disbelief. "I don't know what kind of men you're used to dating in New York, but down here, men do men things, and women do whatever the hell they want! I'm going out the door and I don't care who sees my hard-on, okay?"

Another crash hit the outer wall with such force they jumped.

Lucas pushed Doreen back a little farther and looked down. His erection was completely gone. "Mission accomplished. Doreen, don't come outside until I figure out what we're dealing with. It's probably the storm coming ashore early, but to be safe I want you to stay inside."

Doreen swallowed her objections. "Okay."

Lucas went outside and slammed the door shut.

Doreen waited what she thought was a reasonable amount of time and tried to release the tension from her facial muscles. She had been alone so long she was accustomed to investigating things that went bump in the night. How many times had she wished for someone to go for her? Now that there was someone, why did she wish she could protect him? Why did she wish she'd taken the fireplace poker and run outside first? How long was she supposed to wait? How long was this trust thing supposed to last before she sprinted outside in her bra and his sweatpants?

She went to the controller to activate the blinds, but stopped. The windows were already boarded. Only the kitchen windows were uncovered.

She hurried to the kitchen's bay windows and tried to see Lucas but couldn't, and she walked back into the den as the door opened. Rain splashed her chest and arms as he dashed inside, his head down, dragging in a boxy object.

"Let me get a towel." She hurried into the lower bath and came out with fluffy yellow towels. "What is it?"

"One of two lawn chairs."

"Hitting the house like that? Where'd they come from?"

He stepped back outside and returned with the other chair, locking the door behind him. "Davenport Villas. Stamped right on the back."

"We can return them, right?" She dried his arms while he dried his face and neck.

"A little difficult, but yes. They're in Miami."

Lucas shook like a wet dog. He was soaked to the skin.

"Oh, my goodness. How'd they get here?"

"The current and wind." He looked concerned as he tried several channels on the TV. When he got no reception he turned on the weather radio. Static.

"Is the house damaged?" Doreen asked him.

"Yeah, but not badly. Luckily, I can fix it after this passes."

"Yeah," she said, relieved, "that is lucky." God bless Angel, but her uncle hadn't been able to fix anything and he'd relied on her to learn to be handy. She'd hated that at first, but those skills had made her self-sufficient when she needed to be.

The satellite finally picked up a station. "Tropical Storm Brennen is gathering strength in the Yucatán Peninsula, but all eyes are on Hurricane Ana. She is still on course to strike the Florida Keys with a direct hit.

Cruise ships have been grounded, and officials are asking citizens to help board passengers for a night or two. All of the hotels have reached full capacity. If you have the accommodations, please lend a hand. You can call the television station or report directly to the dock."

Lucas rounded the counter, touching Doreen's waist. "Come on. We need to get to the store and get the rest of the wood up on the windows."

"Lucas, we should help out."

"I don't want strangers in here." He pulled off his shirt and went into his room. Doreen followed, standing at the door.

"Hey, come get this T-shirt."

His closet was the size of her bedroom and luxurious, with mahogany and glass drawers and cabinets. She could tell he'd built it with Emma in mind. There were separate sections for his and her clothing, shoes and boots, hats and purses, formal and informal clothing. Small vanity mirrors were situated in the middle over drawers so they could each accessorize and talk to one another as they got ready for their day.

A part of her was jealous that she hadn't known of this additional surprise, even though the other part of her knew she was being irrational.

Lucas's side was one quarter full. The woman's side was empty. He handed her a pair of boxers and went behind a screen and pulled on dry jeans. "That's the best I can do, sweetheart."

"I would have left while you changed, Lucas, goodness."

"Girl, I'm not shy, but you're already blushing. I

don't want you to pass out." He came around the screen and put his wet clothes in a hamper then he had her against the door before she could blink. "Besides being beautiful, this is a safe room in the storm. If we ever get separated, come here. Don't wait for me. Get in here, pull all this glass from these shelves and stow it in these cases." He showed her several small boxes. "Put them under the bed and then lock and bolt this door, okay?"

She nodded, watching how he secured the door. "That's just for worst-case scenarios, right?"

"Right." He kissed her cheek. "Did you know kissing your neck was almost as exciting as kissing your lips?"

"No," she said. "I've never kissed my neck or my lips before."

She could barely meet his gaze for staring at his lips.

"You're such a smart-ass. I'm enjoying getting to know all about you. What happened in the kitchen…" His gaze melted her resistance, but his quick smile enticed her. "That was erotic."

She played it cool. "If you say so."

"Are you telling me you've had it hotter?"

"I don't play the comparison game. I just don't want to get my hopes up that something meaningful can develop between us when you live so far from me."

"I fully understand, but I don't think that's a problem."

Despite everything that had transpired, Doreen felt incredibly grounded. "What's changed?"

"Nothing yet, but things will."

He seemed to be studying her, but she kept quiet,

her gaze on his Adam's apple. She wanted to wrap her lips around it and stroke it with her tongue. "You're so sure."

He turned his head and his gaze fell to her lips. He nodded. "I am."

She felt her pulse beat harder, turned on by his confidence and machismo. She wondered whether he'd try to prove his point now, right here in the closet.

Lucas's words told her he wouldn't. "You're so lucky we have errands to run, or I'd have you in every room in this house."

She didn't doubt him for one second. But that was the problem, as lovely as it was. She'd let him. "What about helping out the cruise people?"

He closed up a little as he walked her back to the kitchen and retrieved a bucket that held flashlights and candles. Doreen watched his hands as he checked each one to make sure the batteries worked. Though they'd just gone to the hardware store the day before, Lucas wasn't a man who seemed to ever be unprepared.

In his BlackBerry handheld device he made notes on what he needed. Doreen liked that, but she wondered what he needed from a woman. He seemed to have everything taken care of.

She put her hands on his and made him look at her. "These won't be your garden-variety strangers. They've been checked out by the cruise line."

"Cruise lines don't do background checks."

"We can choose a nice couple. I'm a good judge of character. I'm still here, aren't I?"

"You want a spanking, don't you?"

The throbbing started again under his serious tone and intense look. "Not really, no."

"I'm going to figure out that look and then I'm going to do really naughty things to you."

Doreen wished she had on several more layers of clothing. "I'm trying to be serious here. People need our help."

"What if they're thieves?"

"Cruise ships have tons of security cameras. If there's a criminal element, they won't let them go stay with innocent civilians. Then they'd be liable. Besides, what could they steal? The echo of my voice?"

He looked around and she could see the concession in his eyes. He folded his arms. "Okay, but where will they sleep?"

"Oh." The throbbing intensified. "Fine, they can take my room. I'll share with you."

"Well, then, hell, yeah, we can have strangers over." His voice had taken on this seductive tone that made her legs feel like noodles. Navel licks? His hands and him, in and all over her? She wouldn't want to leave Key West, either.

"Why do you look like that? What's going on in your head?" he asked.

"Nothing." Doreen headed for the stairs. "I'll be down in fifteen minutes."

"Come here. That look means something." Lucas caught her by the wrist and brought her to him. His hand caressed her stomach and her back and she tried not to squirm. "Tell me."

"Tell you what? That we need to go? I need a shower

and some new clothes. And pajamas, since we're having company."

They'd gotten as far as the bottom stair, and a key in the front door startled Doreen who grabbed his shoulder. "I'm not dressed!"

All Lucas could do was stand in front of her as Stephen and Terrence rushed in.

"Lucas, get the hell up!" Terrence bellowed from behind Stephen.

"He's got company," Stephen said, staring at Lucas and Doreen.

"Right, Emma. I forgot about that," Terrence said, shutting the door and shaking rain off himself like a golden retriever. He hadn't looked up yet, but Doreen didn't need to see any more.

"Not Emma," Lucas and Stephen said simultaneously, while Doreen wished she had been faster on her feet to avoid this embarrassing moment.

No one spoke or moved.

With nowhere to go, Doreen shrank behind Lucas's back. She wasn't bold enough to march out in her bra, shake hands and introduce herself. Tears burned her eyes and she was in serious danger of melting into a heap of brown goo.

"Turn around, you uninvited knuckleheads," Lucas told his friends, who about-faced immediately. "This is Doreen."

"Nice to meet you." They sounded like schoolboys, but she didn't wait for better introductions, and sprinted up the stairs and into her room where she caught her cell phone on the second ring.

"Doreen Gamble." She held her forehead, sitting on the bed.

"Ms. Gamble, this is the airline. We have a seat available on flight 545, leaving today at ten this morning from Key West to New York LaGuardia."

"A seat? Today? In this weather? Is that safe?"

"Yes. It'll probably be the last flight out of Key West for a few days."

Doreen looked up to find Lucas in her doorway. "You okay? What's up?" he asked.

"The airline has a flight at ten. Can we get there?"

"If you hurry."

He hadn't hesitated or paused. Then he asked the question Doreen had already asked herself. "What are you going to do?"

"I'll take the flight."

Chapter 9

"What the hell is going on here? Yesterday you were engaged to Emma and today you've got a half-naked woman in your house."

Lucas had ushered Stephen and Terrence into the great room and offered them a seat on the floor where they could talk. While Terrence had been sleeping sporadically due to the hurricane and looked like he didn't believe what was going on, Stephen looked disappointed. Though he hadn't really liked Emma's snobby attitude and had always cautioned Lucas about a woman who would never visit Florida, Stephen had always spoken well of Lucas's commitment to the relationship.

"I can't believe you're stepping out on Emma."

"I'm not, Stephen. You know that's not me."

"You're crazy, right? How do you have another

woman?" Terrence demanded. "You don't even have chairs. Who is she?"

"Doreen Gamble. She's Emma's assistant. That's not true. She *was* Emma's assistant."

Terrence burst out laughing and Stephen looked like he'd been kicked in the head by a mule. "Dude, T is right, and you know I never agree with him. You couldn't have Emma, so you're banging her assistant? That's nasty."

"I'm not banging her, and I broke up with Emma before I started anything with Doreen. But I've known Doreen for the past eight months. We talk every day."

"How'd you get to be with Doreen?"

"We got to know one another while renovating the house. Emma was never into the whole decorating thing and delegated the task to Doreen, who has a natural talent for it. All of this is her. She doesn't know that I know, but I do. From the wainscoting to the sconces in the bathrooms. We only got to meet face-to-face this weekend. She's a good woman. Smart, funny, beautiful, and I like her."

"This wouldn't be you getting back at Emma for never coming down here to see you? That's a dangerous game, and it's one people play consciously and unconsciously. Both of you could be trying to get back at Emma for the same reason," Terrence reasoned. "Because that's exactly what I think it is. I couldn't make this up on the radio."

"I'd better not ever hear this or there won't be a hole deep enough for me to bury you."

"Boy, my woman will have you strung up on an

electrical line for messing with me. I got it like that."
Terrence walked around the great room with his chest
out like he was a superhero.

"Man, go get your balls out of Sherri's purse and come
sit down," Stephen told Terrence, and the three laughed.

Terrence walked into the kitchen and over to the
stove. "Say what you want. Sherri and I are different
people after spending so much time at the station. My
baby takes care of me, and I take care of her. I'm not
ashamed to admit it."

"Could you play 'Let's Get It On' any more? What
the hell were you two doing?"

"Taking care of grown folks' business. That's our
theme song and it seems to be working. People aren't
fighting and they're making love. That's what we want
in these terrible times," Terrence said with a smile so
tender Lucas knew he was in love. "So how'd you get
with Ms. Lady upstairs, Lucas? I've got to report this
to Sherri correctly." He pulled down a plate and dished
himself up some rice and pork chops.

"That's our dinner." Lucas poured him some green
tea over ice, and T looked at him like he was seriously
out of his mind.

"She's changed you for real. That better turn into
a Heineken."

"It's eight o'clock in the morning. You only want a
beer 'cause you're eating dinner, fool."

"Riiiight," T said, taking a swallow of his tea. He
walked into the great room and yelled over his shoulder,
"Stephen, you need to get some of this. It's good."

"I'm not drinking anything green."

"That's the last of it. Anyway, Doreen and I talk every day, sometimes by webcam, and we've been doing this for eight months. We talk about the renovations on the house and everything else. She knows paint, sinks, rugs, wainscoting, wood, granite and marble. And what she didn't know, she learned, then she came back with great ideas—and she was open to *my* ideas. We talked every night, sometimes for hours. When I picked her up from the airport, we drove through town and she recognized all the houses I'd told her about. The first one I'd renovated, the ones I've been wanting to buy and fix up.

"When we got here, she was in awe of this house. She loves the kitchen and that was a surprise, especially since she suggested it. The real surprise was the master closet, and I thought she was going to pass out in there."

"You did her in the closet?" Terrence asked as he ate dinner. "You're a real fast worker, aren't you?"

"No, I showed her the closet, you knucklehead. And will you stop telling her to make ice? She thinks you hung the moon. 'Holy Terror said this, HT said that.' It's driving me crazy."

A wide grin split Terence's face. "Where is this lovely woman? I want to welcome her to the family."

"Shut up," Stephen told him. "I called you yesterday and you didn't mention her. Why not?"

"I was in the shed cutting wood. I wasn't trying to keep secrets, but I have a lot to do since I let my crew go home early. Ana blew lawn chairs up on the house this morning and damaged the wood. After I drop her off, I've got a ton of things to do."

"What about Emma?" Stephen asked.

"Honestly, that was a technicality, I realize now. We wouldn't have worked out. She wouldn't have ever left New York, and I don't want to live there. Mom is here and so are you two. You're my family and I'm not leaving. It's been over for months, but I'm not the leaving type. I felt if she came down here, I'd try to make it work, but she didn't show up. Instead, she sent Doreen down here to break up with me."

Terrence reeled back. "That's nasty. That sounds like her, too. I hope you told her about herself."

Lucas shook his head. "I should have called it off long ago and I didn't. I'm equally at fault. So it's over and I have a chance with Doreen, if I don't screw it up. Not like Stephen and Mia. He charged her for her dead daddy's land. Did you know that, T?"

Terrence gave Stephen the evil eye. "You don't deserve her. She's a nice lady, too."

"She'd already lost it," Stephen said as his defense. "I'm giving her easy payments."

Lucas laughed.

"Mia loves me and we're working it out. Don't judge me," he told them. "We don't know what you're doing to Sherri when you play ten commercials in a row."

Terrence pointed his pork-chop bone at him. "Then you're stupid and a bad cop."

They all fell over laughing.

"Doreen had to stay over last night because flights were cancelled, but she got a call from the airline a few minutes ago. They have a seat on a flight out this morning."

The words were harder to say than he realized. He

felt as if he were back in his playhouse with his sixth-grade friends and they were deciding how they were going to get him out of having to leave Florida for the summer to spend two months in New York.

"So let me get this straight," Terrence said. "You've talked to Doreen five days a week for eight months, more than you've talked to either of us or the woman you were supposed to marry. Doreen came down here and did the honorable thing and broke up with you on behalf of your ex-woman."

Lucas smiled. "And she brought gifts for all the guys and gave Horatio a six-week internship in her office in New York."

Their expressions softened. "She did that?" Stephen said. "Tell me more about her."

"I don't know anything about her father, but she lost her mother young to a heart attack. Her uncle Angel raised her until she went to college, and then he passed away."

Terrence sucked wind through his bared teeth. He had a soft heart, though he was a former professional football player.

"And she's got good friends in New York, but she's pretty much on her own. She does volunteer work and works at Regents Cable."

"And she likes you." Stephen looked at him hard. "You shouldn't mess with her, unless you have already."

"I made a guy mistake yesterday, and instead of getting all crazy on me, she reminded me who she was. Then she fixed me a sandwich, put on this pink rain slicker that she bought and brought it to me in the shed. I know it sounds silly, but she's a different kind of woman."

They were convinced she was a good woman, though they seemed to doubt his intelligence now.

"But you're letting her go." Stephen tapped his knee and both men helped him up. He'd been injured recently rescuing a tourist from a ravine. He walked to the foyer and put on his long raincoat.

"Stephen, when are you going back on active duty?"

"Not soon, but they grounded some cruise ships. I'll be over there later."

Lucas shook his head. "I've already heard about that today."

"I'm not finished eating, bruh," T told Stephen.

"Hurry up. We still have to get to the grocery store, and I thought you had to get back to the studio."

"You're right, I do. If you're so into Doreen, how're you letting her leave, Lucas? Your women don't seem to want to be down here, and you don't seem to be able to find anyone in the Keys. Hell, we might have job openings at the station down here, but I'm not saying another word about there being jobs all over the country. If I were you, I'd find a way to get her to stay. I wouldn't be Mr. Nice Guy encouraging her to go back to New York." He looked up at Stephen for support. "You need to be convincing her that the best thing for her is right here in Florida and that's you, 'cause once she leaves she isn't coming back. They never do for you, apparently."

There was something strangely ironic to his statement. In college Lucas hadn't been able to get rid of women. They'd been falling out the woodwork, but now T had a point. He couldn't keep one if he offered free Hermès bags.

Emma's Christmas present was still upstairs in the closet. She'd told him a hundred times to hold it for her, she'd get it on her next visit. Only she'd never managed to get down here to claim it.

Lucas's thoughts returned to the woman in his shower upstairs. The woman whose voice had replaced his fiancée's as the last female voice he'd hear each night before he went to bed.

"How can I stop her? She said she was taking the flight at ten."

"So what would be different about the two relationships? Different woman, same office, same situation. Nasty," Terrence assessed.

"She's different. You have to get to know her, man. She's special."

"If you want her, you need to find a reason for her to stay." Terrence put his dish in the sink and rinsed it.

"I say just ask her," Stephen advised. "Forget all this 'gotta be in love' stuff. It's the weekend. She doesn't have to work until Monday anyway, so what's the harm? Besides, it's foul that her boss put her in this situation. Just be careful."

"I will." Lucas walked them to the door. "What did you come by for?"

"I almost forgot," Stephen said. "There were some reports of looting at the senior condos so I looked in on your mom's house and it's fine. Since we were over here, we thought we'd stop by."

"I appreciate you looking in on her place. I'm glad

she's not here for me to have to worry about. I can't half keep up with her and her friends."

"Cairo, right?" Terrence asked.

Lucas nodded. "Then somewhere in Greece. She just better not come back with another tattoo. I've had it up to here with that."

Stephen nodded. "Well, we're out of here now."

Lucas stopped him at the door. "Before you leave, do me a favor and check the back door on Ms. Lucy's house."

"We'll check the house," Terrence said, answering for Stephen. "All right, we're out. I'm heading back to the station for the duration of the storm."

"You guys be safe out there and just tell me if you need anything. I've got my radios and cell phones on at all times," Lucas told them.

Knowing the dangers, they hugged each other.

"You need a heavier raincoat," Stephen told Terrence on their way out of the house.

"Are you my wife?"

"No, but you still need a heavier coat. Lucas, I need another umbrella. Lift the garage door up." Stephen told him. Lucas went to the garage and let the door up, shaking his head as he went back into the house to check on Doreen. Terrence and Stephen had been friends for so long they fussed like old women.

Their advice rang in his head and he wondered how he could convince Doreen to stay.

Before he could outline a plan, she was descending the stairs.

"I'm ready."

"Is there anything I can do to change your mind?"

"Lucas." Her look said it all. She was leaving. "I need to go while there's a chance I can get out of here."

He got her slicker and opened her door so she could get in the truck. The rain was relentless, the storm promising to show the island its fury. Though it had a woman's name, it promised to be no lady.

He backed out and started down the street, dodging the pothole that had opened up from too much water and not enough maintenance crews to fill the softening roads. Lucas stopped at the red light and drove down the next street, picking up the pace, knowing the line at airport security would be long and crowded.

He headed through the office park shortcut, gaining a few minutes, and was back in a neighborhood when the pop and drag of the front tire surprised him and caused a squeal from Doreen.

Instinctively, Lucas reached out and stopped her forward propulsion.

"Don't worry, it's just a flat. I have a spare. This will only take a few minutes. Don't get out of the car."

Chapter 10

Doreen didn't feel right sitting in the truck while Lucas changed the tire in the driving rain, but he just might have delivered that spanking he promised if she got out again. He'd been at it for a half hour, and she realized there was no way she was going to make her flight.

Her eyes burned with unshed tears and her chest was heavy with disappointment. Now she wasn't going to get out of Key West, and to make things worse, Lucas hadn't spoken to her since she said she wanted to leave.

The day had started well. She had never had a near orgasm in a kitchen before. She'd never been with a man who'd so carefully taken care of her needs and not his.

Lucas was incredibly unselfish, but she couldn't stand taking orders from anyone, and he loved giving them.

Twice he'd ordered her to follow instructions and

expected her to do as she was told without any discussion, and she was at the breaking point.

And now he wasn't even speaking to her. Everything was different. Sitting in the truck on the side of the street, too scared to tell him to forget the airport, was ridiculous.

She was going to be the director of special events, for goodness' sake! She wasn't going to get bossed around, she *was* a boss!

Doreen put her shoulder into the door, pushed it open and accepted the battering rain.

She got to the front of the truck where he was still struggling to get the tire off. The lug nuts were too slick for him to get a grip on and he was frustrated.

"Didn't I ask you to stay in the truck?"

"You *told* me to stay in the truck, but we're not going to make it. Can we just call someone now?"

"You saying I can't fix my own damned truck?" His eyes were angry, and his tone was one she'd never heard before.

She watched him as he stalked to the back of the truck and pulled out another wrench, put it over the nut and spun it.

Doreen tried for a more diplomatic approach. "You probably can fix your truck under better circumstances, Lucas." She coughed on a mouthful of water and turned her face turn downward. "But maybe not today."

"I told you to stay in the car." He walked around her and threw the wrench into the bed, and it made a terrible clanging noise. He picked up the tire.

"I don't want to stay in the car. I don't want to

leave. I won't make it. Can you please stop moving?" Doreen did the unthinkable and burst into tears.

"Why are you crying?"

"Because you're angry with me. I said I wanted to go home and you stopped talking to me. Now I can't go home and you're still angry."

"I'm not angry with you."

"Now you're lying," she yelled.

He leaned the tire against the truck. "Okay, I'm lying. I don't want you to go."

"I'm not going!"

"I know!" he yelled back. Lucas put his hands up. "Can we please talk about this in five minutes? Please?"

"I'm not getting back in the truck until you're done," she said, still crying. Doreen wanted to control herself, but she didn't know what to do. Her cell was in the car. She couldn't even call a taxi without looking like a fool.

"Why not? You won't get wet."

"I'm already wet!"

He looked around like he couldn't win for losing. "Okay."

She kicked a puddle of water at him. "Don't you dare smile at me when I'm upset."

"Fine," he said.

"Fine!"

As he went back to work on the tire, she turned her back on him and covered her mouth, trying to gain control of herself. Water streamed down the inside collar of her slicker, into her shirt, wetting her chest and back. More tears came, and she knew she was making a fool of herself.

A big black Labrador mix ambled down the street and Doreen stepped back.

Lucas looked up and saw Domino, the neighborhood stud dog. He didn't aggravate anyone except the parents of the female dogs he impregnated.

The last lug nut finally popped off and Lucas changed the tire. Doreen was circling the For Sale sign on some people's grass and suddenly ran to the porch. Domino thought she was playing and made a beeline for her.

Lucas considered bailing her out, but he'd offered for her to sit in the truck and she'd refused. When she screamed his name, he whistled and Domino came right over, soaking wet but happy. "Where you goin'? To see about your girlfriend?"

Domino barked once and took off running without a backward glance at Doreen.

Lucas threw the flat tire in the back of the truck and rescued Doreen off the porch of the elderly couple who'd come outside to investigate the ruckus. She'd taken refuge behind their rocking chairs.

"Were you going to let that dog eat me?" she asked.

He didn't even answer her but pulled two towels from the drawer beneath her seat and let her wipe her face. Then he started the truck and drove away, relieved that she wasn't leaving.

Pulling out his phone, he dialed Terrence. "Hey, it's me. I just saw Domino running down Justine Street, heading toward Westerly Place. Will you remind people again to bring in their animals? Domino, too. And tell the road crews there's a buildup on Hartwick Avenue. The drains are covered in debris. Doreen didn't make her flight. We're heading to the store and then back to the house. I'll talk to you later."

Lucas hung up and turned to Doreen. She looked waterlogged. "Domino's the friendliest dog in the world."

"Says you," she said testily.

"Yes, says me." He stopped in a parking space at the grocery store, noticing how packed it was. "What's wrong, Dorie?"

"You're angry and you stopped talking to me."

"I'm not going to lie. I don't want you to leave."

"I have to go home sometime," she said.

"No, you don't."

"Lucas," she sighed. "Yes, I do. Regardless of what develops between us, I still live in New York."

He remembered the smell of the street, the crowds of people and the death of two of his friends when a work crane collapsed on top of them. He didn't have good memories of New York.

"I don't want to deal with that again."

"Don't you think you should have thought of that before you let me straddle you and you kissed me like a starving man? This is what I was talking about. Men get you invested in them and then want to change the rules of the game," she said softly.

"I'm not changing anything."

"You most certainly are, Lucas. And I'm going to feel like a fool."

"Not if you give what we're feeling a real chance."

He touched her face and she leaned into the palm of his hand.

"I like New York because it's what I know," she said softly. "Just like Stephen and Terrence are your best friends, Alicia and Cynthia and Pinky are mine. They know my history."

"Who you went to the prom with?" he asked.

She squeezed her nose and nodded. "Percival Johnson."

"I already hate him."

She giggled. "He was a head shorter than me, and his mother made him wear his mouth guard in the car on the way there."

"I love her." He caressed a lock of wet hair off her face.

"My job at Regents is important because it's what I've striven for. I worked for it and I earned it. I don't want to walk away from this dream job and look up six months from now and realize I should have taken it."

"I can say that wouldn't happen, but it does all the time," he said. "I hear you. But I'm not going to stop wanting you. My first reaction was anger back there. I admit it. I didn't want you to go."

"Okay."

He smiled at her. "This is the weirdest fight I've ever had."

"Don't be angry with me for wanting to see my apartment and wear clean clothes and my own underwear. My whole routine is changed and I don't mind that, but this is a little different. And the whole dog thing notwithstanding, I saw how hard you tried to get me to the airport, and I appreciate it."

"I was angry about that, too. My tires never go flat. That was crazy. Four nails in the tire like that. It's like somebody put them there."

"You just had a run of bad luck," she said.

He caressed her cheek. "No, it means you were meant to be here. Say you'll stay a little longer."

She looked in his eyes, seeming to search them for the right answer.

"What is it?" he asked.

"It's just me. I have to be careful."

"What does that mean, baby? No, I know." He took her hand in his. "It means you're taking a big risk with no family and friends down here to give you advice. We came together in an unusual way, and if you had your girls around they might warn you to be more cautious. Do you think you should be here?"

She wasn't crying anymore and he took that as a good sign. "Yes and no."

He didn't want to get out of the car now. "Am I moving too fast?"

"It felt right until reality walked in with a key and called me Emma. Then it felt really wrong," she said, biting her lip.

"That was awkward," he admitted. "But I explained everything to them, and when you're ready, I'll introduce you to them the right way."

"I'm glad they know so it won't happen again. But we won't be running into anyone soon, will we?"

He shook his head. "No. But I want you to stay until next week."

"I kind of have to now."

He wanted to take her in his arms so badly, but holding her hand was good. He kissed it. "They're good guys. Like the brothers I never had."

"Terrence and Stephen," she said. "What did they say about me?"

"They said I shouldn't let you go. They both had a hard time winning their women over. Falling in love isn't easy for any of us, so for me to tell them I've met someone when they were expecting Emma, they're questioning my judgment. They're also taking this seriously."

"I would question your judgment, too."

Lucas shrugged. "They know I don't make hasty decisions. I don't do anything without giving it the consideration it needs, so they know me well enough to know I don't do stupid."

"I don't, either," she told him.

"Do you think love has to be difficult?"

Lucas asked the burning question that Stephen had raised to him long ago. He'd been challenged in getting together with Mia.

"Love can be very hard." Doreen wiped a stray tear from her cheek. "That's why it ends in divorce."

"Why does that make you cry?"

"It doesn't. A lot of things about love are hard, Lucas. Living in different places. Different religions. Different values. It depends on the couple."

Lucas laced his fingers with hers. "I once heard a famous mogul say he worked hard all day at his job. He didn't want to come home and work hard at love."

"Moguls are known for being married a lot."

"Maybe. But there's some truth in his words. You may have to work at marriage, but it shouldn't feel like you're pushing a bus."

"I agree with that."

Lucas grinned. "Come on, let's go inside. I'm going to buy you some panties."

She smiled back at him. "You may have just won me over."

Lucas took off his seat belt. "This is the best part about fighting. Making up."

"Do you not see me? My hair looks like a raccoon's tail, and I don't have any makeup on."

"For a raccoon, you sure are fine. Can I kiss you?"

He didn't wait for her to answer, but got real close so he could feel her.

She nuzzled his neck, and when his lips found hers it felt right.

When their lips parted, he smiled at her. "I'd like to take you out later."

"During the hurricane? You want to take me on a date?"

"Yes. We'll be in the house, but, yes."

Doreen couldn't help herself. She felt herself blushing. "I'd like that."

Chapter 11

The store was packed with perspiring shoppers, some anxious, others resigned to the fact that Hurricane Ana would hit Key West again and they needed to get as many groceries as possible.

The mentality was one he'd grown accustomed to, living in the Keys. Storms were a common occurrence and it was better to be prepared for the worse, even though more often than not nothing serious happened.

Today, however, the shoppers believed the hype. Their carts were filled with bread and water, crackers, peanut butter and jelly, and any other food that could be consumed without the need of a stove.

As they waited in a line to get a cart of their own, Lucas consulted his BlackBerry handheld, but Doreen got impatient.

"There's a cart behind your truck. Nobody's going to get it, so I'll get it and we won't have to wait."

He looked at the packed lines and the distance to the truck. "I'll get it."

"It's not in Spain. I can get it."

Lucas caught her by the arm. "I said I'd get it."

She barely suppressed her exasperation. "Lucas, I don't mind." With that, she ducked into the rain and took off.

He watched her sprint across the lot, her legs stretching as she leapt over a puddle. In some ways he was sure she was enjoying herself. She was finally moving at her own pace, even though she was alone. New Yorkers moved fast, accustomed to each other.

He climbed houses like others did mountains and she went to spinning class to burn frustration, when what she probably needed was to make love for a good, long time.

That was why she had to run out into the rain instead of waiting patiently for a cart. Standing and waiting was driving her crazy. She needed to move quickly.

He was learning her.

Lucas knew how he would have her their very first time. Hard and fast. Too bad it wouldn't be in front of a crowd. The idea made him smile.

"You going crazy, standing there smiling all by yourself?" Mrs. Carmichael asked him.

He turned to see a friend of Ms. Lucy's. "No, I'm just waiting for my friend," he told Mrs. Carmichael.

"You don't have any manners?" she asked, watching Doreen run back with the cart.

He laughed at the eighty-six-year-old woman. "I've got sense, but she needed the exercise. She's happy now."

Soaked but smiling, Doreen ran back to Lucas with the cart. "Got it!"

Mrs. Carmichael scowled as she tied her rain bonnet under her chin. "No manners," she mumbled under her breath.

Lucas smirked as he introduced Mrs. Carmichael, who wasted no time chastising him again.

"I offered to go outside," Doreen said, giving him a sweet you-owe-me smile. "I didn't mind."

"He still knows how to be a gentleman. I gotta go. It's poker night. You wanna come by? I'll be glad to take your money, Lucas."

Lucas wasn't into giving away his money. Not even to little old ladies. Though rumor had it Mrs. Carmichael was richer than Oprah Winfrey. Nobody really knew.

"No thanks, Mrs. Carmichael. I've got to board up Ms. Lucy's place, but I'll get by real soon. Take care, now." He helped her load her van, then returned to the store.

He and Doreen waded through a sea of carts, harried adults and happy babies. Doreen seemed like a frustrated Cubs fan. She was hurrying to get to a seat when the game wasn't starting for another three hours.

Lucas took his time, leaning on the handle of the cart, knowing she'd learn to slow down. Everyone did once they got used to the Florida culture. He helped old ladies get food from top shelves, and talked an old man out of having a hurricane cookout.

"You're a regular Boy Scout," Doreen said as she took his hand and steered him toward the beverage aisle.

"Nothing wrong with helping out your fellow citizens," he said, watching her load their cart with wine. "How much of that are we going to need?"

"How long is the storm going to last?"

"A couple days."

"I don't like thunder and lightning," she told him. Her expression was apprehensive, but when her lips thinned into a smile, he could tell she was trying hard to be brave. "We might need a few more."

"Get red, too. It goes with darker meat. Be right back."

Lucas hurried off and found the essentials he'd promised her and a few other items.

He looked for Doreen where he'd left her and she was gone. Strolling down the aisle of lotions and soaps, he heard his name. "Was that Lucas McCoy I saw a few minutes ago? I hope he didn't see me." Lucas recognized that voice. It belonged to Traylor Dean.

"That was him. I've been meaning to get by to see if he's going to list his mother's house. I heard she's in Egypt. I can sure use the business." That was Suzetta Charles.

"Don't ask him anything," Traylor hissed. "You real estate people are so desperate sometimes. I hope he didn't see me. He looks so bad now. Girl, I'm glad I got rid of him."

Lucas frowned. He'd taken Traylor out a couple times to dinner, but that was a long time ago. She'd turned into a wacko, having too many stipulations just to share a meal. That was when things had begun to get tight with Emma, so it had been a natural move to end his association with Traylor.

"Traylor, you didn't get rid of him. He told *you* to stop calling *him*. Anyway, I heard through the grapevine he's got a big-time girlfriend-slash-fiancée in New York."

"Where'd you hear that? He doesn't have anything from New York. He's a scruffy, mangy dog. His hands felt like sandpaper and he always looked disheveled. I mean, can't he pick himself up a little bit?"

"Excuse me, but I'm disheveled, too, in all this rain. My hair won't hold a curl, and my skin hasn't seen the sun in eight days."

Lucas remembered Suzetta even better now and was surprised that she'd defend him. She and his mother hadn't gotten along for a while. There'd been a dustup about the seniors and youth taking care of the babies in the church nursery, and each side had wanted to win. She and his mother had locked horns but had eventually worked out an agreement.

"Suze, this isn't about you," Traylor blurted obnoxiously. "If Lucas McCoy wants a woman he's going to have to do a lot more than pretend to have a girlfriend from New York. The man needs a makeover."

"I need a makeover," Suzetta complained, sounding distant and distracted. "You're just mad he didn't choose you. I think I'll get some sardines."

"You won't have a husband if you do. Lucas was a big-time architect like his father in New York, but what does he become? A lowly refurbisher of tract housing." Traylor sounded pouty. "He gave up that big money to come down here and tear up floors and rip out toilets. I watch those home-improvement shows, and the things they have to do are disgusting. Please, he's nuts!"

"All money is green, Traylor. I'll meet you in line. I need feta cheese, cherry tomatoes, tuna and crackers."

Lucas studied his hands. They were calloused and white where they should have been smooth and soft, like when he'd worked in an office. She had a point, although he took issue with the "mangy dog" comment.

He considered himself to be like his house. A serious work in progress, and not like the abandoned and broken properties of the foreclosure era. He might not get action every day, but he wasn't hurting for attention.

Lucas spotted a sample bottle of lotion and squirted a healthy amount into his calloused palm. He sniffed it and drew back. Gardenia. Really? On his hands?

"Excuse me." He heard the familiar voice one aisle over.

"I need those Magnum condoms. The ones with forty in the box."

He laughed so hard his eyes watered. What was Doreen doing now?

"Yes, that box of condoms right there," he heard Doreen exclaim. "Thank you. It's Suzetta, right?"

"Yes. Have we met?"

"Thanks, no. But I'm Doreen Gamble. Nice to meet you. As for you," Doreen said, her voice turning edgy, "I don't think my fiancé, Lucas, and I should waste a moment of the storm sitting up when we can have so much fun doing all kinds of other things. Don't you, Trailer Park?"

"It's Traylor Dean," Traylor barely mumbled.

"I don't really care. You should learn to keep your voice down when you're talking about another woman's man. Or better yet, shut the hell up. *I'm* his woman from New York. Any questions?"

He thought Traylor was clearing her throat, but over the din of the crowded store, he couldn't really tell.

"Good," Doreen said.

Lucas couldn't help himself and laughed aloud.

"Honey, where are you?" Doreen asked, sounding sweet again.

"One aisle over. Getting some lotion for my hands."

"Don't you dare. I like them just the way they are. Suzetta, again, a pleasure." He heard Doreen and her squeaky boots coming toward him.

To save face, Traylor became verbally indignant the farther away Doreen got, but Suzetta silenced her. "She's why he has a fiancée and you don't. I'm heading to the checkout in five minutes. Bye, Lucas," she called out. "Call me about your mama's house."

"Not selling Mama's, but I've got another one we can talk about. Later, Suzetta."

Doreen walked over and unloaded her purchases into his cart. "I hope she wasn't a friend of yours."

"I have sharks that are better friends. Girl—"

"What?" she asked, her hand on her hip.

"You sure know how to get Brooklyn on somebody, don't you?"

She wagged her finger at him, fighting a smile. "Don't you start with me," she said, as he pretended to bite her finger, then drew it between his lips and kissed it.

"No woman has ever defended my honor before. Thank you."

A sexy blush crept up her neck to her cheeks, and

for a moment she seemed to be at a loss for words. "I don't like people like her." She blew out a big breath. "You're welcome."

Lucas leaned down and kissed her cheek. Doreen put her hand on his chest before sliding it around and patting his back.

"Come on. I saw an old man in the produce section. If he says one thing you don't like, I'm tripping him."

Lucas laughed so hard, people stared at him, but he didn't care.

The store lights flickered and Lucas headed straight down the aisle for the checkout, beating out two other careening carts with harried shoppers behind them.

"You're going to have to get some clothes without me. Two shops down is kind of a general store. If we lose power, they're going to close up because they can't use their cash registers."

Doreen looked up at the lights. "They only blinked."

"Yeah, but that's like a warning," he explained. The lines had filled with people once again and the rain slashed the ground with intensity.

The lights flickered again. Lucas dug into his pants pocket and gave Doreen his credit card. "Go down there and tell Beverly you're with me and I sent you down there to get some clothes. Give her my card. Even if the lights go out, she won't kick you out until I come to pick you up."

"This isn't junior high. I can pay for my—" Doreen stopped as Lucas pulled out his calculator and started adding up his groceries.

She watched him, her mouth open. "You're not serious."

"If the lights go out, this is what the store is going to have to resort to. Go!"

"Okay." She took off running, and he watched her sprint into the store just before the power went out in the entire plaza.

Chapter 12

By the time they reached the docks, hundreds of people crowded the pier, giving the term *organized chaos* new meaning. Tired couples from the cruise ship sat in lounges aboard the ship waiting for their names to be called, while Lucas and Doreen stood in equally long lines to claim the couples who had to evacuate the liners.

The whole concept had a foster-child feeling that left Doreen with sad reminders of the three days she'd had to spend in foster care waiting for Angel to pick her up after her mother had died.

Lucas tugged her hand. "We can leave now, and you can show me what you bought in that huge bag of yours. I've got wine, fruit, food and me. Plus, I owe you a big thank-you for handling Traylor." He tugged her hand and laced his fingers with hers. "Ladies' choice."

"What's my prize?" she asked, looking him up and down.

"Us, picking up where we left off this morning. Or we can take it deeper."

Doreen rubbed her neck as she stepped up in line. "I thought you were going to suggest a mani/pedicure from Betty down the street."

Lucas eyed her lips. "Do I look like the type of man who'd go to Betty down the street for anything?"

The twinkle in her eye indicated she was playing with him. "You might."

"And what would I get from her that I couldn't get from you?"

All of the sensual dreams of last night came rushing back. Lucas's hands all over her body. The roughness making her skin feel alive after not feeling anything for so long. They weren't scour-pad rough like that idiot woman made it seem. They were rough enough to titillate and had aroused her to the point where she'd had to work out this morning or she'd have been climbing the walls by now. Or climbing him.

"I assure you that Betty doesn't have anything on me. One day you might find out."

"Don't tempt me, woman."

"Traylor did mention that your hands were like sandpaper. They don't feel so rough now."

Lucas must have played his fair share of poker because his face gave no indication of his emotions. He bent down as if he was tying his shoe. The next thing Doreen knew, her pant leg was up and he was caressing her calf.

Tendrils of unfulfilled need shot straight to her groin. "Too rough?" he asked innocently, stroking as high as the fabric would allow him to go.

He was completely aware of his power of seduction, and his work-worn hands worked overtime on her skin.

He was seducing the goodness right out of her!

They were in a public line of several hundred people and he was feeling her up. To everyone in line, he looked like he was massaging a stiff muscle or assisting with a cramp. Doreen was the only person who knew her panties were now moist from his ministrations far south of their intended goal. Her breasts even responded to the combination of his touch and the glow of fire in his eyes.

She tried not to groan aloud, but her knees threatened to give way, and had his palms not been locked around them, she'd have been on the floor, doggie style.

"You're going straight to hell," she hissed, but the words fell short of angry, tumbling into the orange-y glow of sultry, and had the setting been different, he could have grasped her hair and ridden her to a fiery, thunderous orgasm.

Doreen limped forward when Lucas slid his other hand up and caressed her ass. If anyone was looking, it would have been clear that they were amorous lovers.

The couple behind them must have caught the entire exhibition, because they encouraged Lucas to get her out of there and finish the job. Doreen burned, not from embarrassment at being caught but from knowing others witnessed their byplay and the thrill it gave her.

When he finally stood and put his arm around her

neck, Doreen relaxed her head into his arm for a second. "Are you always this bad?" She tried to clear the seduction from her throat.

"Much worse."

Goodness, her nipples were hard, and she was thankful to be holding her slicker over her arm. She took a giant step away from him, trying to gain control of her hormones and her common sense.

"Is there anything you won't do?" She minded Lucas in her personal space because he had the power to overcome all her objections for them to take things slow. Her body was quick to overrule her mind as it had just done, so she had to keep her distance. With Lucas, that was almost impossible.

Maybe they should get two couples.

"I believe in complete pleasure, Dorie," he said, capturing her hand and bringing her back to his side. He was already working his talent again. "I won't stop until we've both achieved it." He pressed his lips to the sensitive skin next to her ear.

Her body responded with a shiver and she stepped back, but he easily slid his arm around her waist and held her against him. "Where you going?"

"Nowhere, Lucas." Her hand fell to his chest and she felt his heartbeat.

"You bring out the bad boy in me. You feel so good. Don't you know that? Don't you know how much beauty and power you possess?"

Her gaze traveled over the fullness of his lips to the hard set in his jaw. His neck was strong, and in her dreams when he was on top of her, his muscles stretched against tight skin, making her want to surrender whatever she had to soothe him.

"Don't you know it's going to be my pleasure to please you?" he said.

She regarded him for several seconds. "I'm getting the idea."

The crowd had increased to about six hundred people and the noise level had risen. In a way, though, they were in their own little world, and Doreen was able to experience Lucas's subtle caresses because no one had the time or inclination to pay attention to them.

They'd been told the air-conditioning was on, but because the ship was docked, the air wasn't pumping at full capacity. All around them Good Samaritans like them fanned themselves with the forms they'd had to complete.

Finally, they approached a long table of volunteers who took the form that Lucas had completed, and his ID.

The lady, a tiny blonde named Francesca, copied his form and gave him a sheet of information. She then stood up so she could be heard above the din. She referred to the paper in her hand first. "We're anticipating the storm will last for a night or two, and we're praying there are no aftereffects like in previous storms.

"We ask that you tune in to WLCK for all updates as to when to bring your couple back to this location so they can reboard the ship. If there are emergencies, notify us at the contact number immediately."

"I don't like this." Lucas handed the form to Doreen, who gave him an encouraging pat on the back.

"They have to say these things, but nothing bad will happen."

Francesca confirmed Doreen's sentiment. "Nobody wants any trouble. These people want to go on a cruise, that's it, and they want to get out of here as soon as possible. You're doing a good thing by helping us out. The couples have been instructed to be nice and helpful. They know if they commit any crime, they'll be punished to the fullest extent of the law. That being said, your couple is Mr. Brandon Ingram Goodfellow and his wife, Mikaylah. Good luck. There's a deputy at the door who is giving out business cards."

"You say that like we're going to need it." Lucas looked ready to walk out the door.

"We seriously hope not."

Lucas nodded. "I see my friend, Deputy Sheriff Stephen Morales. I'll stop by and say hello."

"If you'll wait just about two minutes, the Goodfellows will be right down."

"Have them meet us over by the deputy."

Lucas's hand sought hers and they walked toward his friend, who seemed relieved to see a familiar face.

"Hey, Lucas. I checked on Ms. Lucy's place and it's locked up tight."

Lucas nodded. "Good. Strange thing. My tire had four nails in it." He regarded his friend closely. "You wouldn't know anything about that, would you?"

"That's a felony and I can't commit a felony."

"That wasn't a no."

Stephen elbowed him to shut him up and looked at Doreen. "Ma'am, Lucas doesn't have any manners. I'm Deputy Sheriff Stephen Morales."

"I know he doesn't. I'm Doreen Gamble. Nice to *officially* meet you."

Stephen had the grace to look embarrassed. "If Lucas had told us he'd found a better woman, you'd have never seen this handsome face."

"Aren't you almost married?" Lucas demanded. "You and Mo think you're the biggest studs since Domino, and you couldn't be more wrong."

"That dog is in big trouble. Four dogs are already pregnant. If I catch him, he's getting it cut off. No more for Domino."

Doreen grinned.

"As for me," Lucas teased, "I think Doreen should decide."

Her eyes widened. "Who am I to challenge what God created?"

Stephen tapped Lucas on the shoulder. "This is the one, man. She's beautiful and intelligent." He turned to Doreen. "If he messes up, you come to my house, and my girlfriend and I will have this boy on his knees begging for forgiveness."

"Really?" Doreen put on a sweet smile and gazed at Lucas. "I'll keep that in mind."

"Be careful if you wanna eat later," he said.

"Now you're threatening not to feed her? You've really slipped in my eyes. After all I went through to keep you two together," the deputy sheriff said, all smiles.

"I knew you did something to my tire."

"I did not. I'm a cop." He smiled and held on to his belt with his thumbs. "I prayed for you. She's already a touch on the thin side and you know how we like to do down here. We cook out on the weekends and before you know it, pow-pow."

Lucas shook his head at her. "He's as crazy as Terrence."

Doreen looked down at herself. "There's nothing thin about me."

"Stephen, I got up and she was in the great room letting some man from the TV yell at her, making her do some boot-camp exercises. He said squat, and she did it. Drop and give him twenty, and she did it."

The deputy burst into gales of laughter. "Hell, I need his number. Maybe he can get Mia to do something I tell her. I'm in charge of this island, but I ask Mia for something, and she looks at me and I melt. I'm liquid in her hands."

Lucas shook his head. "You've got it bad."

Doreen's face was warm with embarrassment. "I thought you couldn't remember how long you'd been standing there," she said to Lucas.

"I was mesmerized by your—"

Stephen elbowed Lucas in the ribs. "That look on her face means if you want sex anytime this year, you'd better not finish that statement."

Lucas tilted his head back as the lesson seeped in. "I can't say that's going to happen anyway, Stephen, so we'd better change the subject. Do you know anything about the Goodfellows?"

Stephen looked up at couples up on the deck. "Most of 'em seem nice, but they're tired and fussy from sitting here and not being on a cruise. Others want to gamble and they're anxious, so don't take any of the ones hugging the machines. You sure you're not going to need any help with Ms. Lucy's house? They've been using prisoners to shovel sand all day and four tried to escape. I couldn't be part of the capture. Instead, I had to come down here."

"I'm sorry," Lucas said sincerely. "There'll be other escapes."

"That's not what we really want."

"Of course not," Doreen agreed, giving Lucas the eye and a quick shake of her head. He shrugged, as if asking how you were supposed to console someone who wanted to catch bad guys.

They both looked sad for Stephen.

"Say, where you from?" Stephen asked her.

"New York."

"Strangest thing. I haven't ever met a nice New York woman."

She smiled. "Until me."

"That's right. Until you."

A couple walked through the crowd of people, unapologetically bumping into others and arguing like two Chihuahuas.

On cue, the man stopped in front of him and looked up. "I'm Brandon Ingram Goodfellow and this is Mikaylah. Everybody calls me Big. They call her Mikaylah."

The couple looked alike, both barely five three. The black woman had curly hair and a big smile, while he wore a green plaid short-and-top set over a sleeveless T-shirt, with socks and white sneakers.

"Nobody calls you Big. You made that up for this

trip," Mikaylah told her husband. "Your name is Brandon Goodfellow, and I've been calling you that for twenty years. I'm not about to change now. Can we leave? It's hot in here."

Brandon Goodfellow seemed unfazed. He took his time and regaled Lucas. "We were both in the circus for thirty years, me as an animal trainer. Now I'm an electrician, good with my hands. She's a housewife. Good if you give her specific instructions one at a time. We have a special diet. We eat gluten free. It's something new we're trying."

"You're a windbag, Brandon," Mikaylah told him.

Lucas's smile was feral. "So you're not going to die if you have food with gluten?"

"No, but that's not what we want," the short, balding man said. His chest seemed to punctuate his statement like an exclamation point.

"Now you listen to my rules." Lucas spoke coolly and quietly. "You eat what we serve or you don't eat. If you complain at all, I'll bring you back in the middle of the hurricane. We're not your maids or your servants, but we understand that you're stressed so we'll do our best to make sure you're happy. If you're in agreement, we'll all get along just fine. You got it?"

"I don't know if I like your tone," Brandon said.

"Then you can stay here," Lucas told him. He turned to walk away. "Doreen." He wasn't asking her to leave. His tone brokered no such question. It was, in fact, a command, in a tone he'd never used with her before. Every female instinct in her told her to yield to him, and she wanted to respond, but she couldn't.

She wouldn't speak out against him, and she wouldn't verbally confront him, either.

Instead, she did something she'd never done before. She kept quiet and simply looked at him.

Stephen stood by, a look of interest on his face, like he was a referee in a death match. He'd call the winner.

Doreen took a step closer to Lucas to narrow her field of vision. She wanted him to see only her. Her body met his, his shoulder lining up between her breasts, his hands tangled with hers.

Lucas's fingers twitched and Doreen caressed his hand with hers, drawing circles on his palm with her finger. His gaze seared hers as he looked intently into her eyes.

Words were unnecessary.

He was only doing this for her. And she loved him for it.

Doreen blinked and the question of clarity rose in his eyes.

His hands tightened until she opened her eyes again. He wouldn't accept her hiding. No matter what, they would be together tonight and always until she left.

The slight tilt of his eyebrow asked for confirmation and she agreed. Doreen slipped up onto her toes, held his face between her hands and sealed their deal with a gentle kiss.

"Thank you."

He hugged her tightly and pressed a kiss to her cheek. "Thank me later."

Lucas shook hands with Stephen, who looked like he'd officiated a barbecue wedding.

Doreen, who shared her seat with Mikaylah, shushed the quibbling couple several times during the ride home, as Brandon kept arguing from the jump seat. By the time they got home Lucas had a wide grin on his face and didn't even come into the house, but went straight to the shed and then to Ms. Lucy's.

Doreen made the Goodfellows as comfortable as possible, feeding them and getting them settled in the great room on the floor with movies, but Brandon's bad back caused him to complain, and Doreen had no choice but to take the movies and Goodfellows to the upstairs bedroom.

That meant there would be no distraction from being with Lucas. She cleaned the kitchen, finishing the bottle of wine from dinner, watching for him out the garage door and through the rain, unable to see a thing.

Worried it was too dark, Doreen pulled her rain slicker off the garage peg and got a flashlight from the bucket. She slipped her feet into flip-flops, wishing Lucas had seen her cute floral skirt.

She'd have to wear it for him another day. She tossed the slicker over her neck, when she heard the Goodfellows starting up again.

"Excuse me," she yelled up to the second level.

She almost regretted taking in the travelers. Almost. That was, until she anticipated having to share Lucas's bed in a few hours.

Chapter 13

Lucas never walked through his house wet. Coming in soaked to the skin, he preferred to undress in the garage and leave his clothes in the laundry room next door.

He'd grown so accustomed to living alone, walking naked from the laundry room to his bedroom was normal. But this time was different. This time Doreen had his hand, and she was guiding him to his bedroom.

Fat curls cascaded past her shoulders, nearly touching the halter top that left her shoulders bare. He could make out only the faint movement of her butt in the thin skirt, but it was enough of a teaser for his thoughts to jump ahead and imagine himself driving into her while holding her ass in his hands.

They slipped into his bedroom and he closed and locked the door, something he'd never done before.

But he wouldn't be disturbed by his houseguests. Not even the raging storm could stop him.

Inside the bathroom, she stopped him in the center of the spacious room.

He'd been selfish with the design and the minimalistic approach to the room. There were two sinks, a walk-in steam shower and a tub, the toilet in a separate room. The same Italian-designed sinks from downstairs had been installed in this bathroom as well, but it was the six-by-five-foot black chromatherapy Jacuzzi tub that was his pride and joy.

And now the magnificent tub, built for two and filled with steaming water and rose petals, commanded his attention. Doreen had lit white candles and placed them on clear ledges all along the wall. She'd suggested he install them months ago, and he'd been apprehensive, but he'd trusted her judgment and had made only a few modifications.

And now he was glad he had. She'd found just the right fragrant votives to complement the bathroom and had transformed the room into a sensual haven. *Their* haven. He'd never thought it possible. She'd even lit the gas fireplace he'd installed in a last attempt at decadence.

"It's beautiful," he whispered.

"Thank you."

Doreen didn't look into his eyes as she concentrated on opening each button of his shirt before struggling to pull it from out of his jeans.

He lifted up his shirt. Her gaze darted to his, and it was as if her eyes seared him. His dick stretched his wet jeans tighter.

"Let me do it?" she asked him.

Lucas relaxed. "Okay."

Along the way she'd lost the flip-flops and was barefoot, a smile of satisfaction curving her lips as she worked his shirt from his pants.

Only then did her soft hands slide the top down his left arm and then his right. His shirt fell and slapped the floor. When her mouth was close to his shoulder, he leaned into her. "Bite it."

Again, her gaze didn't quite meet his, grazing him with heat somewhere near his cheekbone, but she bit him, and he sucked wind between his teeth. "Oh baby, you're gonna hurt me."

She did smile big this time and popped up on her toes for a kiss that lingered like the scent of jasmine in spring.

She tasted of wine and warmth and sensuality, and as his tongue crossed with hers, desire zig-zagged up his groin to his stomach. She was making love to his mouth, her lips and tongue telling him of her longing.

He'd never been kissed like this before, and he held her there, enjoying the journey through this unchar-tered and gentle place.

She caressed the back of his head, and when he thought she was separating from him he became filled with irrational longing, and he grabbed her arms and used his lips to capture her by the chin.

He'd seen animals mate on nature shows, their foreplay of nipping one another playful and gentle, and he understood that visceral animalistic instinct to claim one and make that one their own.

Purring started deep in her belly, and he put his arms around her knowing she felt that magnetism, too. When the moans were nearly out of her, he sealed her mouth with his so they released into him.

The pressure of her mouth lessened and she eased off her toes, her hands busy at his waist. Her fingers tangled with his as they battled for who would get his belt loosened first.

"Let me."

"I can do it faster," he told her.

"I don't want it fast," she said, as she slowly began to push his jeans over his butt and down his legs.

"If we keep this up, there'll be no bath," he said.

"I know." Pulling off wet denim was a challenge but Doreen got behind him and Lucas wanted to protest as she had him step out of his clothes. "If I face you, I'll want to lick every part of you, and we both know how that will end. I'm leaving now so you can bathe, and I'll be back in a few minutes. But before I go, I want to tell you something."

"What is it, baby?"

She put her cheek on his back and held him close.

"I don't have any diseases or do any drugs, but I want us to use condoms."

He brought her hands to his lips and kissed them, relieved it wasn't some terrible news. "I heard you in the store buying a box of forty. You think we're gonna need all of them?"

Her mouth moved on his back. She was smiling and planted little kisses down his spine, then she hesitated. "You want to tell me anything? Talk about anything?"

He admired her straightforwardness. He'd never had this conversation with a woman before. He'd always taken control of the protection, but Doreen… she was unique and special.

"Baby, I don't have anything. No diseases, no drugs, no down low, no secrets. Never have, never will. And I have a box of forty in my closet and a couple in the nightstand, hoping a brotha would get lucky, so we've got over eighty. Okay?"

She nodded, her hair tantalizing him. "I'm glad. Get in the tub and I'll be right back."

Her hands were flat against his chest, her body against his butt. "You're not going anywhere, unless it's into the tub with me."

"Lucas, I already bathed and did my hair. I want you to warm up and relax after working so hard."

He pulled her wrist until she was in front of him. "You're not leaving me now. Bathe with me."

"I have food for you, and wine."

"It will keep, Dorie. Baby, I want you with me." He put her hands on his dick. "It's nothing to be afraid of."

"Who says I'm scared?"

Rain trembled down the solar panels. "Then why are you trying to run?"

"I'm not. I had the whole evening planned."

He brought her close until her hands and his hardness were all that was between them. "I did, too."

Lucas worked her halter off, leaving her breasts free, and then he unzipped the skirt and spread his hands, separating fabric from skin until it slipped off and pooled at their feet.

Reaching inside a drawer, he pulled out a pack of hair clips.

"For me?" she asked sweetly, and she kissed his jaw.

He could get used to her. "I bought them today at the store."

Lucas tried to capture all of her hair and clip it, but her long curls fell and the clip leaned precariously to the side.

Doreen giggled and kissed his Adam's apple, his collarbone and his neck. "May I help you, Mr. McCoy?"

He caressed her arms, looking at the clip. "Please do. I can build a house, but I can't clip hair."

As soon as she pulled up her hair, Lucas captured her breast between his lips and gave her something to think about. She practically writhed as his mouth worked her sensitive nipple over. She smelled faintly of vanilla and flowers, and like a bee, he wanted to occupy her, to have her all to himself.

The flimsy scrap that was her panties was the last to go, and then he stepped down into the water and brought her with him.

The hot water had turned warm and Lucas sat down, bringing Doreen down between his legs. She pulled a fuzzy washcloth into her hands, squeezed soap on the center and began to wash him.

"You're spoiling me," he said, his hands riding up her hips. "I feel like I'm in a movie or something. Like all my wishes have come true."

She washed his neck and bent to kiss his lips. "All of them?"

"You're here, aren't you?"

She kissed him again, this time her tongue leaving his mouth tingling. He wanted to get closer, but anytime he brought her hips toward him, she pulled back and soaped more of him.

Finally he submitted to her ministrations, watching as her hands and arms moved in the quiet water. Only one level of jets was going, the water moving like the hot springs he remembered from Durango, Colorado.

"You're gorgeous," he said, getting bubbles of soap from his leg on her breasts. When she'd thoroughly soaped him, leaving only his sex untouched, he took the cloth from her hand and finished the job, then slid under water and rinsed himself off. When he came up he grabbed some towels.

Doreen watched him. "You ready to get out?" she asked.

"Not yet."

He walked back to her side and dropped the towels behind her and lifted her into his arms, his hands cupping her butt. "I love your breasts."

He rocked with her in his arms, for the first time hearing the music that was coming through the flat-screen TV on the wall.

"I noticed," she said. "Are you hungry?"

"Only for you."

The firelight from the built-in gas fireplace played tricks with her eyes. "Don't say it if you're not going to mean it."

"I know you feel all of me. What part of me do you think is playing?"

Their gazes held until he couldn't take it any longer.

"You still need convincing?" He walked up the steps and out of the tub, giving her a hand up, then wrapping her in a silver terry bath sheet. They headed out of the bathroom, and as he was about to clear the doorway Lucas grazed the wall panel, and fans extinguished the candles, the tub drained and the built-in music speakers increased in volume.

"That's magnificent," she said, her eyes wide.

"That's technology," he told her, taking her to his bed.

Doreen let the towel fall like a cape from her shoulders and he sat down on the bed with her in front of him. She was unashamed of her body and he loved that.

He'd been so methodical in his planning for Emma and had bought all her favorite lotion and creams, but he'd tossed them this morning, knowing he'd share this bed with only one woman.

Still, there were things he didn't know about Doreen. Her fragrances or her lotion, and he wanted to know so she would feel comfortable in his home.

"I wanna put lotion all over you. Touch you." Lucas couldn't resist tasting the chocolate cone of her nipple that was enticing him.

He heard her sharp intake of breath. "Go ahead," she said as he sampled her breast.

"I don't know what kind," he said, burying his face between her breasts.

"Bobbi Brown Beach lotion," she exhaled into his hair. "But the kind you bought at the store today is fine. Hurry, before we dry out."

Lucas was off the bed and back in half a minute. He stumbled out of the closet when he saw all of the decorative pillows on the floor and Doreen stretched out facedown on the sheets.

"I know I've died and gone to a much better place."

He kneeled on the bed between her legs, rolling on a condom.

She kicked her feet, looking at him over her shoulder. "Take care of me."

Lucas removed the lid from the bottle and focused on her arms and hands, moving down her sides and back. Then he moved to her legs and feet, kissing her toes and ankles, using his hands and tongue to learn her body. He rubbed her calves along his chest, her thigh across his knees, and when he drove his fingers inside her, she wriggled, pulling away, her wetness making him crave her.

He sank one hand between her cheeks and held her still while the other hand got to know all her womanly folds. She reached for the side of the bed and pulled hard, and Lucas used his foot to stop her from getting away. Her breathing changed.

He sank his fingers deeper into her, and she grunted and looked over her shoulder at him. Her hands dove through her hair, meeting the clip. She grasped the plastic and flicked it onto the floor, her hair tumbling down her back as she arched into his penetrating hands. Her hamstrings tightened and released the closer she got to orgasm, and a guttural noise wrenched from her throat that he knew was "Please."

She reached for him and he denied her, working his hand in her, his thumb against her clit. She buried her face in the bed, her left arm tight against her side.

Climax eluded her, and he knew he had to possess all of her before she would completely let go.

He pulled her by her spread legs until she was high enough for him to taste her and shoved pillows under her chest. Then he sank his mouth onto her folds and made love to her with his lips and tongue.

With one hand he roamed her legs and butt, which he adored, and with the other he pumped her, until her climax was imminent.

She came, and her scream of release brought absolute joy to his heart. She grabbed his leg and held on to him and he pumped his fingers inside of her as she came down.

"I want you."

"You're not too sensitive?" he wondered aloud, pulling her into his lap and kissing her collarbone and neck. He could barely keep from penetrating her, but he wanted her to accept him completely.

"No," she said and kissed him, wrapping her arms around his neck. "Not too," she managed before he directed his manhood into her. She whimpered and moved in his lap.

Lucas watched the way she enjoyed herself. There was an unabashed abandon to this woman that made him want to take her to new heights.

"Kiss me," she breathed, capturing his jaw and ravaging his mouth while she gently scratched his back with her nails.

Her whole lower body tightened the deeper he pressed, and she writhed on top of him.

Lucas fought coming, grabbing her butt and bring-

ing her to him in a swift movement that had them connected completely, fully, sex to sex.

As if he hadn't had enough, she leaned back and
braced her hands on his knees. Seeing her like this was
almost too much with her breasts tantalizing him and
her sex gripping his. He slipped his hand between
them, knowing he'd bring her to climax quickly.

Doreen moved to get up and he held her there,
keeping her body open and vulnerable. She gritted her
teeth, accepting his thrusts, calling his name and
begging for release, and when her walls closed around
him like a second skin and she gushed, he brought her
against him and roared his own release, his lips
against her heart.

Doreen scooted out of bed as Lucas slept, and went
into the bathroom. He'd ravaged her and he'd laid
claim to her body like no man had ever done before.

And now she loved him.

She was in big trouble. She found a towel to cover
herself and went into the toilet room and sat on the
commode. She used the bathroom and flushed.

Squeezing her eyes shut, she rocked on the balls of
her feet while the automatic toilet sprayed water on her
entire private area, and then blew her dry.

The whole experience was mind-boggling. The
toilet cost well over a thousand dollars and Lucas had
been convinced that it was the wave of the future. She
got up, unconvinced.

What was she going to do about him? She'd never
come so much in her life. Now that she knew what a

real orgasm felt like, she knew she'd been having baby orgasms for the past ten years.

Everything about him was amazing. His body, his house.

Her body was so relaxed, sleep threatened to overtake her.

As soon as they announced the storm was breaking, she'd start putting some distance between them. She found a washcloth and gave herself a sponge bath in the sink, then found deodorant in the cabinet and swabbed some on.

She sniffed the fragrance and drew back. This wasn't hers.

Emma's.

Putting the deodorant back, she closed the cabinet and walked back into the room, sliding into the bed. She stayed on her side, but Lucas found her and tugged her into the fold of his body.

Honestly, it felt so right there, she didn't want to move. Her nether region ached for him, but it hurt from all the attention, too. She hadn't been with a man in nearly two years, and all the activity had left her sensitive.

His roughened hand massaged her hip and he sighed in his sleep, his abs curling against her back, his hair tickling her butt.

Lucas was a beautiful man, his physique that of a man in his vain early twenties. Guys their age were starting to get that "I'm thirty" pouch, but he carried his weight in lean and bulky muscle in all the right places.

"Would you go to sleep so I can get some rest?" he said softly.

Doreen tensed at being caught. "I thought you were asleep."

"You're thinking so loud I can't get any rest."

"Sorry."

He rubbed her stomach, something he'd started doing that she loved. "I'm really listening to the weather. It's getting bad out there."

"Does the island have an evacuation plan?"

"Yes, they do."

"What is it?"

"Leave on the last plane. Yesterday. The I-10 is closed, so we have to ride it out, baby. We islanders know what to do and we're doing it. You made food and I have other nonperishable provisions. We'll prepare more water jugs, though I have some in the laundry room, and we'll move everything into the closet."

Doreen turned over and faced Lucas, who leaned up and rested his head on his hand. "My house is built higher off the ground and has never ground-flooded," he assured her. "But there have been houses that have been damaged by trees, and other houses have washed away. Those are the things you can't prepare for. We have to be ready for anything."

Doreen felt herself tearing up, but she reminded herself she was in bed with Lucas and she was safe, for the moment.

He must have sensed her fear because he caressed her shoulder and stroked her hair. "That room has been reinforced to withstand anything. Even if the house blows apart, the room won't come down. If we have to evacuate, we go to that room."

Lucas kissed her gently. "There's no need to worry. How about some more sex to get your mind off the storm?"

"I'm sore, you sex-starved man." Even as she said these words, she put her leg over his, liking the pressure of his leg on her sensitive area. Oddly, she felt herself becoming aroused.

He brought his leg higher and lay back down, caressing her back. "That's right, damn it, and I'm doing my job. Now stop worrying and go to sleep so I can wake you up with an orgasm."

"I'm not going to know how to act when I get back to New York and you're not there with me."

He was quiet a while. "You don't have to go back."

"I do, sweetheart."

"We'll talk about it later."

Lucas suckled her breasts, never taking the pressure off her core. "Relax," he whispered. She lay back, accepting the pleasure he gave her until she realized the next day had arrived.

The pleasure of his mouth awakened her and she slid from sleep into consciousness, a delicious orgasm already tickling her legs and sliding up her back. She arched into it, calling his name when it hit her again, like the sheets of water smacking the house.

The climax continued to overpower her even as he climbed her body, stopping along the way to love her navel, and then her left nipple.

She backed up on one elbow, but scooted forward just as he grabbed her hips. She knew he hated her moving away from him, but she wasn't. She was just giving him room to stretch all of that fine muscled, black manliness on top of her.

There was a greediness to the way she wanted him, like a hunger that couldn't quite be fed, and she would give him anything to get close to meeting that need. Any part of her. All of her.

He lay on top of her, his face buried in her neck, his body not moving, and she grazed his face with hers.

"Sweetheart, you okay?" she finally asked him.

"Better than okay, baby. I want you so badly, I had to slow down a minute."

Pure feminine power surged through her, and she was almost heady with her strength as a woman. She was Cleopatra and he was her Julius Caesar—but their end, she hoped, wouldn't be tragic.

Her love for Lucas soared and she embraced him, bending her leg out at the knee.

"Oh hell, you're starting trouble," he moaned, sounding so sexy that if she'd had on clothes, they'd have melted off.

"You started a fire. You have to put it out." She dragged her nails over his nipples.

When she took the little pebbles into her mouth, his erection jumped against her thigh and she knew he understood the immense pleasure he gave when he did the same thing to her.

"You're going to be sore," he said.

"I have all day to recover," she said, as she pushed him over and took him in her mouth.

The light was barely discernable from outside, the

blinds closed, the windows boarded as she pleasured him.

He was long and thick and she loved the feel of him in her mouth. Though she was no expert, he certainly seemed pleased when he grabbed her, laid her down, rolling the condom on at lightning speed, cupped her ass and plunged into her.

Doreen accepted each thrust and closed her eyes.

"Look at me, baby."

She opened her eyes and saw love emanating from him.

Doreen grabbed his arms, making him collapse on top of her as she blasted her orgasm all over him, relishing his release seconds after hers.

Chapter 14

"It's about time you got up. We're hungry."

Brandon Goodfellow looked angry, and Lucas wished again that the little man would walk into the storm and disappear.

But he stood in the kitchen with a red plaid short set on, a replica of yesterday's green outfit, and glared at Lucas.

"Good morning, Mikaylah. Brandon."

"Morning, Lucas. I took the liberty of starting some coffee. I hope that was okay." She winked at him and sipped from her cup.

He smiled at the kindhearted woman, whose wink meant she knew what he and Doreen had been up to. "That's just fine. Let's see what I can dig up for breakfast."

"I'll be glad to help," Mikaylah offered. "Will Doreen be joining us?"

"Mind your business, nosy woman," her husband snapped.

"You mind yours, Brandon. At least they're having fun instead of being a party pooper. You know, you should learn how to make the best of a bad situation. Life is about how you live it. It's not about all the disasters that happen to you. I'll bet this hurricane will mean something different to Doreen than it does to me. When's she coming out, Lucas?"

"She'll be out in a minute," Lucas said loudly before the fight could get any bigger. "She's getting dressed."

Brandon had planted himself on one of the two bar chairs at the counter and wasn't moving. He was playing lord and master very badly.

"Mikaylah," Lucas said, "can I bother you to go upstairs and look in the first door on your right, which is the linen closet. There are tablecloths in the top middle drawer. We can use those to eat on. The furniture wasn't delivered on time because of the storm, so I apologize for not being able to seat you comfortably."

"Lucas, that's all right."

"Also, Brandon, if you could bring the blankets down. We may have to use them in an emergency."

"No."

Mikaylah was nearly out the kitchen when she looked back at her husband. "Honey, did you say no?" She sounded as if she didn't believe him, but Lucas was sure of what he'd heard.

"I sure did. We don't work for them. We're their

guests, and so far they're not very hospitable. If you used the other half of your brain, Mikaylah, even you could do a better job than them."

"Brandon—" she started.

Lucas put the eggs and bacon on the counter. "Mikaylah, if you'd check on Doreen, I'd appreciate it."

Her eyes were troubled. "Sure, Lucas."

He waited until the bedroom door clicked closed and he went around the counter and turned on the radio, listening to the updates on the storm.

Hurricane Ana was pummeling the island, but the worst was still to come. They were expecting it to increase in strength to a Category Two before it was over.

"The storm is worsening," the newscaster said. "You don't want to be outside right now. Take cover."

Brandon folded his hands and glared at Lucas. "What are you going to say to convince me to want to help you out?" he groused.

"Nothing." Before Brandon understood what was happening, Lucas had him by the collar and had shoved him out the deck door and into the driving rain, locking the door behind him.

He turned on some hip-hop music to drown out the man's bellows and knocks to get back inside.

Lucas opened the garage door. He needed to get that wood up on two of Ms. Lucy's windows. He washed his hands and started the bacon. After putting it in the oven, he rewashed his hands, taking his time, unlocked and opened the door.

"Brandon, in my house, we respect women and we speak to them with respect."

Brandon's shoulders had been hunched up, but they dropped. Lucas waited for an answer.

"Okay," he finally said.

"I realize I may not have asked as politely as I could have. Brandon, could you *please* bring down some blankets in case we have to use them in an emergency?"

The man looked contrite and scared. "No problem."

Lucas let him in and they heard the women gasp.

"Brandon, why were you outside? You're soaking wet," his wife wailed.

He walked inside and through the kitchen, his head down. "I was checking out something for Lucas."

"Oh, my God, let me help you."

"No, thank you, Mikaylah. I'll take care of it. I'll get the blankets right away." He took off his shoes and socks and walked up the stairs barefoot.

"I'll get those tablecloths," Mikaylah said, following her husband.

Wide-eyed, Doreen met Lucas in the large kitchen. "Do we need wine with breakfast?"

"I'm cool, baby."

"You're angry."

He considered denying it, but stopped himself and nodded. "I'm angry. The little shit wants to be waited on, and he insulted us and his wife."

"So you put him outside?"

Lucas watched Doreen. "Yeah, I did."

"Okay, don't get tough with me. I'll have to throw some Brooklyn on you, then we'll both have a problem." She kissed his cheek. "Shake it off. It's over. But you have to remember, he doesn't work for you, boss man. You're used to issuing commands and having them followed, and obviously when he didn't do that, you went all Frank Lucas on him."

"Who's that?"

"Denzel Washington played Frank Lucas in *American Gangster*."

"You saying I'm a gangster?"

She pointed to the watery footprints on the floor. "Baby, do I have to say it?"

Lucas rubbed his head, got some paper towels and wiped up the floor, feeling less than pleased with himself. "He *was* remorseful when he came inside," he told her.

Doreen looked apprehensive and checked the bacon.

"I got the bacon," he snapped.

"Okay, Frank," she said over her shoulder, as she took the bowl of eggs and started cracking them.

Mikaylah hurried in. "Lucas, Brandon said he'd clean the water up. It's like he had a religious experience or something outside. Anyway, how about I set up in the great room? You know that Holy Terror is a funny man. He's on the radio upstairs talking about how you should be nice to one another and love one another. I told Brandon he needs to take a lesson before he's loving only himself."

Lucas smiled at Doreen, and in a silent language they agreed to tune Mikaylah out.

"Can we start over this morning?" he asked Doreen.

"Lucas, where's the silverware? I may as well set up a full-fledged picnic. Doesn't that sound nice?" Mikaylah walked off and turned the radio to WLCK, them proceeded to talk back to Terrence.

"I'm fine," Doreen finally answered Lucas after laughing at Mikaylah's motormouth. "I'm thinking we should let you be the brawn of the relationship and I'll be the finesse, okay?"

He considered her proposal, looking at it from all sides and finally admitting that it might not have been a good idea to lock the idiot out on the deck.

"I can get with that."

She sidled up to him and rubbed her breasts against his arm. She knew how much he liked that. "That wasn't so bad, right?"

"Right."

He looked out the garage again and up at the ash-colored sky. The storm pummeled the house now, and the winds had picked up. He figured the storm was making landfall now and the next twenty hours would be rough.

The rain was heavy and steady, but it would only get worse.

"I'm going to finish up breakfast and go check on Ms. Lucy's."

"They won't let her come home in this, will they?"

"Oh no. She's in the hospital and then she's got to go to a rehab center. It'll be months before she sees that old place again. Come here. I like fighting with you."

Doreen buried her face in his neck, glad they were getting to know each others' likes and dislikes, too. If Mikaylah and Brandon hadn't been there…

"You have fun last night?" he asked in her ear.

She blushed and opened the refrigerator, pulling out some onion. "What do you want, applause?"

She put the onion on the counter and got behind him

while he was at the stove fixing strips of bacon on the tray. She started patting him on the butt.

"Yay, Lucas rocked Doreen's world. Haawww. The crowd cheers," she said in his ear, and started giggling.

He slipped the second pan of bacon into the oven and removed the first. He dropped the pot holders and caught her in his arms so quickly all she could do was yelp before his mouth ravaged hers.

Mikaylah came up right beside them and watched them kiss. They had to stop for laughing at the woman.

"Oh, don't mind me. You guys are so cute. I wish Brandon was like that. All he wants to do is get his and then he's done. Nothing for me. Brandon?"

Mikaylah left the kitchen and went upstairs, fussing at her husband for not being more romantic.

"It's going to be a long day," Lucas said, as he dropped kisses onto her succulent mouth. He loved Doreen's hands and how she encouraged him to give her more of what she liked.

"I've never squirted anything before, Lucas," Doreen said softly. "I was shocked when that happened." She wouldn't look at him and he found that so cute.

He made it obvious that he was trying to look into her eyes by stooping down. She finally made eye contact and he made sure he rubbed her thoroughly as he stood up against her.

"I know that look means you're embarrassed, but you've seen my naked ass," he said. Her eyes darted toward the foyer, but the Goodfellows were still upstairs.

"You've seen my feet and my knobby knees," he said, to which she laughed. Lucas intertwined his fingers with hers. "And you're embarrassed because you squirted some love juice on me?"

She closed her lips. "It's never happened before," she whispered. "I was gushing."

"That's right. It was probably all that green tea you were drinking. We need more of that." Thunder shook the house and Mikaylah screamed, running down the stairs and into the kitchen with them.

She hugged them and Lucas couldn't help but laugh, she was so little.

Brandon hadn't made a sound.

Doreen pulled out a box of green tea and Lucas wiggled his eyebrows. "I'm going to get that wood up on Ms. Lucy's and I'll be right back."

Doreen looked at the stove. "Your bacon."

He rushed over and snatched the oven door open. A string of expletives filled the kitchen as smoke poured out of the oven.

"Baby, this is your fault," he said, pulling out the pan with the blackened strips of bacon. His mouth quirked into a smile. "Damn, that was going to be good."

"How's it my fault?"

"I was messing with you."

She laughed at him as he walked to the garage and opened the door then stopped short.

"Mikaylah, go get Brandon," he yelled over his shoulder. "Baby, call Stephen and tell him to send help."

"What's going on, Lucas?" Doreen asked, alarmed.

"There's about four inches of water in the garage and we've got an alligator."

He shut the door just as the animal lunged.

Chapter 15

Doreen stayed in Lucas's room after she called Stephen, who promised to send Pete from the animal rescue center. She didn't know anything about alligators except they belonged far away from her. Mikaylah also stayed with her.

Stephen had told her to call Terrence, too, and as she listened to the radio, she heard him alert everyone that alligators were looking for refuge from the storm. He again called for families to bring in their pets.

"Lucas and Brandon have been out there for an hour with Pete," she said to Mikaylah. "How long does it take to catch an alligator?"

"Honey, we worked with elephants and tigers. Alligators aren't the type of animals you can train." Mikaylah looked worried. "I was watching from the front door, but there's so much rain, I couldn't see anything. I can't believe this is an actual hurricane."

Doreen paced the bedroom then went back into the closet to take down the glass panes from the shelves. She wrapped them in towels and stacked them under the bed, hoping that if something happened they wouldn't get sliced to pieces.

She and Mikaylah worked quickly and quietly, and after the last pane was removed, they wiped their hands on a clean cloth and sat on the bed.

"I don't want to cry," Mikaylah told her. "Brandon would get angry if he knew I was crying. Let's do something to keep busy. Maybe make buckets of water."

Doreen hopped up. "Mikaylah, you're so smart. Better yet, let's fill the tub."

They hurried into the bathroom and Mikaylah stopped short. "It's as big as a swimming pool."

"You're right, it is." Doreen started the nozzles and they watched the water closely. "If there's any sediment, we'll stop it immediately."

"I hope they come in soon. Do you think the alligator is still in the garage?"

Doreen shrugged. "They've been gone so long, I hope not."

Something hard hit the house and they jumped, grasping hands. "Doreen, I don't think we should push our luck. We have enough for a couple days' drinking and whore baths if we need it."

"What are whore baths?"

Mikaylah pretended to wash under her arms and

between her legs. "That's what my mom used to call washing up."

"You know, I knew there was something special about you the moment I saw you and Brandon."

The women laughed despite their stress. Doreen knew she had to keep busy or worry about what was going on outside. They moved food from the laundry room and all the flashlights and flares to the master bedroom.

Mikaylah's phone rang and she spoke to her husband. "Doreen, they want us to look for duct tape. Brandon said the ropes are too slippery and they need to tape the gator in order to move it safely."

The women tore all the cabinets apart and found a bag full of tape. Ripping off the wrapping, they threw it out the front door and Mikaylah's phone chirped again.

"It's Lucas for you."

She grabbed the phone. "Hi, sweetheart."

"Baby, your phone's dead."

Doreen looked down at it and, sure enough, she didn't have any bars.

"I want you and Mikaylah to go into the closet now," he shouted.

Fear crawled into her and the phone went dead.

"What did he say?" Mikaylah asked.

"Go into the closet. But I don't want to go without him."

"Honey, you'll get over that. I learned that every time I went out on that tightrope and he went into a cage with an animal. Let them be men and us be women. He's trying to protect you. Come on. They'll be happy we did what we're doing. Let's get finished.

Brandon hasn't worked with animals in almost five years. He's not very fast anymore, and if I were an alligator, I'd sure go for the short, fat one first," she said, her voice breaking. "Sometimes I can't stand him, but he's my husband and I do love him."

"I know." Doreen swallowed. She could hear the men yelling at one another.

She and Mikaylah jumped and ran down the hall, heading for the front door.

"What if it's eating them?" Mikaylah asked.

"It's not," Doreen said. "There'd be screaming. Still, we'd better be prepared." She ran into the kitchen and brought some first-aid items to Lucas's room, which was taking on the appearance of a small efficiency apartment.

"I love the spiral staircase. What's up there?"

"A private deck."

"Honey, I think we might need to put some blankets and plastic up there so water can't come down."

"Good idea," Doreen agreed. "I saw some tarp in the laundry room." They hurried to get it, and when they were finished setting up the tarp, Doreen couldn't wait any longer. "It's time for them to come in," she said.

She shared her other slicker with Mikaylah, and just as she yanked open the door the men were coming inside.

"What in the hell is going on?" Lucas demanded, looking at the women.

"We were coming out there to save you two," Mikaylah told them. "We heard yelling a long time ago and then nothing."

"Where's your houseguest?" Doreen asked anxiously.

"Over in Ms. Lucy's garage. Pete will come back

for him tomorrow," Lucas explained. "We checked the place while we were there. Boarded up tight. Thanks, Brandon."

"Good work, Lucas. I've got to change again. Man, we need to put on scuba gear and keep it on."

Lucas laughed, and the men shook hands. "I really appreciate your help. Not a bad alligator catcher. I'm glad that Pete is down the street or we both might be singing a different tune right now."

"Wouldn't want it for a day job, but you're not bad at it, either. I'll be down in a bit."

Brandon headed up the stairs, followed by Mikaylah, who cooed, "You're so brave, Brandon. That makes me really hot for you."

Doreen followed Lucas to his room. She waited until they were behind closed and locked doors before she remarked, "I guess he did have a spiritual experience. You two look like you're getting along."

Lucas stood in the bathroom and stripped everything off. He threw his clothing on the floor and walked into the shower. "There's nothing like facing down an alligator to make you friends. It was really a baby, but all alligators are scary."

Doreen hadn't said a word. She'd seen Lucas naked all night long, but she was suddenly shy about standing there talking to him while he soaped his body all over. She hung up his wet clothes, then walked into the closet. "What do you want to wear?"

"Nothing," he said, right behind her. He pressed her into the cabinet, his hands caressing her backside.

"Do you know how sexy I find your ass?"

"As a matter of fact, I think I do."

"Every time you walk away from me I want to catch up with you and go with it."

Doreen started laughing, unable to believe she was stimulated by his graphic man talk.

"Is that all I am, a piece of ass meat?" she asked, using her gluteus muscles to stimulate him. She'd kiss her spinning instructor the next time she saw her.

"No, baby. Not by any means. You're intelligent and caring and kind to a fault. Look at who's in my house." He slid his hand beneath her cotton top. "Never in a million years would the Goodfellows be my friends. But look at me. Look at you."

She turned around and he couldn't keep his hands off of her. Doreen felt the same way about him.

The look in his eye told her everything she needed to know. "Now, Lucas?"

"Yes, now, love."

"What about them?" she asked, pulling her shirt over her head.

"I don't need an audience, unless you want one."

She smacked his bare bottom and the sound cut through the air.

"Oh, you want to play rough?"

"No," she said, giggling, as he wrestled her to the closet floor on top of the blankets Brandon had brought downstairs. In no time flat Lucas had her jeans off and lay between her legs. He ran his roughened hands up her sides to her breasts and goose bumps rose on her skin.

"Well, where's my reward for wrestling that alligator?" he teased her.

"You didn't wrestle it. You threw some meat at it and ran."

"What?" he asked, incredulous. He slid a hand between her legs and fingered her, making her writhe and moan in ecstasy.

"You see what you make me do to you?" he said. "Take it back."

She shook her head. "Make me."

His eyes narrowed playfully. "Are you daring me?"

"That alligator was really a stuffed animal."

Lucas leaned up in his drawer, put on a condom and rubbed his hands together while Doreen tried to keep a straight face. "Brandon didn't look scared," she taunted him.

"Oh, that's it!"

As if he were really fed up, he pulled her arms over her head, held her legs down with his leg and went to work on her breasts. Even as she tried to get free, resisting him added to the stimulation.

She moaned aloud after every lave of his tongue. Every time his lips left her nipple a sense of loss overcame her that made her arch into him again.

She loved the texture of his teeth, the suction of his mouth and the pressure of his tongue. He knew how to bring out the passion in her, and he was making her feel it all right now. He was setting her body afire. She was powerless, completely at his mercy, and knowing that he was bringing her so much sensuality and daring pushed her forward. She wanted him. All last night, in her sleep. Even now she wanted to open her legs and give him all of her, but he dipped his fingers just enough to tease her but not give her the release she craved.

Finally he trailed his tongue down below her waist and his tongue worked its magic there. Trapped beneath him, she was powerless to do more than enjoy his affection. In fact, knowing she couldn't get away heightened her release. When she exploded, she bathed him in her juices.

But Lucas wasn't done; he didn't release her arms or her legs.

Doreen tried to catch her breath as he moved back to her breasts again, coaxing another climax from her. She thought she'd died and gone on home.

"I'm too big for you to carry me," she said, when he picked her up to carry her to his bed.

"I just wrestled an alligator, woman. I think I know what I'm doing." He put her on his bed.

She could hardly laugh as she scooted over and waited for him to get into bed before she rolled on top of him.

"Aren't you too sensitive?" he asked.

"If you ask me that again—"

"What you gonna do?" he taunted, grabbing her ass, easing his touch. She could tell he was memorizing her body. She loved his hands and how they felt on her and couldn't imagine not having them in her life.

"You'll see," she told him, sitting up. "How do you want it?"

His eyes got bright. "I get to pick?"

"Alligator wrestlers get special perks for saving their lady's life. So, how do you want to make love to me?"

"On our sides. Me behind you, so I can still hold you."

She kissed his lips, having grown to love them. "You sure? I thought you were going to go for you behind me, my butt in the air."

His smile was purely masculine. "Baby, don't tempt me."

He flipped her over and her head smacked the pillow. Lucas kissed up her side and her underarm, and Doreen giggled. "Quit!"

"Alligator rescuer's choice for the rest of the day. I should call Brandon and tell him he can do anything he wants today because he's a hero."

"You don't hear them?" she asked, giggling as Lucas bit her on the side and nipple.

"No." He sucked her breast.

"Shh. Listen to that squeak."

Lucas listened. "Is that them? I thought part of the roof had blown loose."

Doreen poked him in the side. "Come here, silly man. I want to kiss you."

When kissing led to another amazing climax, he held her relaxed body. "Was this way better or the other way?"

"Be quiet, alligator man. You're messing up the mood."

Doreen's phone rang and they looked at one another, surprised. She reached for it and answered.

"Hello? Oh, hi, Emma. What's going on?"

"How are you down there?" Emma sounded so proper and smug.

Lucas slipped off to the bathroom and Doreen sat up in bed, feeling guilty.

"We're trying to stay safe," she replied.

"Good. Listen, is Lucas around?"

"No, he's not. Is something wrong, Emma?"

"Well," her former boss said, "I guess I can tell you. I've had a change of heart. I want to work things out with Lucas. Tell him our engagement is back on."

Chapter 16

When Lucas came back from the bathroom the open phone lay on the bed but Doreen was nowhere around. He picked it up.

"Hello?"

"Hello, yourself," Emma said, sounding happy. "How's it going?"

"Have you been watching television? There's a hurricane hitting as we speak."

"I know that, but you're so handy, I have every confidence that you're going to be fine. Now, about us. I'm sure Doreen told you I want us to be engaged again. Forget the last few days happened and we can pick up where we left off—except with a few concessions on my part. I know there are some negotiating points we can make."

"Emma, no, there aren't."

"There are always negotiating points, Lucas. Now, I know you want me to come down there more, so I'll do that every ten weeks."

Lucas stood there, silent, as the storm shook the house. He listened and prayed. Finally he spoke. "Emma, it's over between us. We're never getting back together again."

He hoped his words would hit home, but he could hear a note of desperation in her voice.

"Lucas, I remember when you loved my 'dirty draws,' to coin a phrase."

"And I remember when you loved me enough to come down here every two weeks, but things have changed. Dramatically."

"You sound different."

Lucas didn't feel right talking to her without clothes on. He went into the closet and saw what Doreen and Mikaylah had done while he and Brandon had been outside. They were the type of women men built lives with. They cared. They were thinking about everyone. Not just themselves. They didn't negotiate weeks. They had done what was necessary—stocked the room with food and supplies in a neat and orderly manner.

He found underwear, shorts and a shirt, and pulled them on even as he heard objects hitting the outside of the house. "I am different, Emma. We were over a long time ago. I guess it took me a while to figure that out. Something has changed for you. Is it the job?"

"Some things have come into perspective."

"I'm sorry to hear that, but—"

"Lucas," she chided, the hint of pain in her voice so clear he could nearly feel it. "You can't spare a couple minutes for an old friend? Your fiancée?"

"Former," he said gently, unable to let her turn back the clock. No matter her current situation, he wasn't going back there with her. But he would give her a couple minutes. He sat on the bed. "What changed?"

"I went on a retreat and had to come back early. The president wants more than just a vice president. He wants a sex toy. A manager from our foreign office believes I should be available to him as well, and he hinted that the president planted that thought in his head.

"I'm so shocked I don't know what to do. I pretended to get ill and needed to return immediately, but I came home to regroup." Disappointment edged her words.

"That's too bad. What are you going to do?"

"Hire a fiancé to kick his ass."

Lucas laughed. "Smart idea. But you might not have to go that far. You have cameras everywhere. Record incriminating statements and make a deal. Let him know that you'll keep the peace if he stays out of your way."

"That could backfire."

He plugged his ear trying to hear above the sound of the rain on the roof. "It could, but you didn't get where you are by not knowing how to play both sides of the game," he told her, rising. He needed to find Doreen. "I've got to go."

"You sure you don't want to make another run at us?"

She wanted a bodyguard, not a husband. "I'm positive."

"It's Doreen, isn't it? She's your type."

"No, it's not Doreen," he said honestly. "It's me. Take care, Emma."

Lucas hung up and threw the phone on the bed. He looked up the winding staircase that led to the enclosed balcony deck and walked up. Doreen was on the patio wearing a shirt of his and a pair of his gym shorts. She'd only found one of his shoes and her hair was wild.

She'd been in a hurry to get out of the room and he could tell she'd been crying. Doreen had a flashlight with her because the lights in the house had been flickering. They still had power, but it was fleeting.

He sat down beside her and she got up and went to the farthest wall. On the love seat made for two, he saw the small earpiece and phone, and he knew she'd heard the call.

Rain pounded the glass and Doreen jumped and so did his heart. "Doreen, want to share with the rest of the class?"

She spun around, her eyes tearful. "I don't want her to love you. I don't want her to know your body. I don't want her to have kissed you. I don't want her to have made love like we've made love, and to know how we've made love, and her to have done that with you, and—" She started crying. "And for her to think she can think about you."

She covered her face and her body shook. "What's happening to me? I want to hit her."

Lucas crossed to her and caught her face in his hands. "You are the prettiest thing in the world, you jealous woman, you."

The house shook with the force of the wind and rain.

"We should go downstairs to a safer level."

"I'm not jealous," she whispered, tears running down her face. "You were so nice to her and I wanted to hit her in the head, Lucas."

He laughed against her mouth. "Aww, baby. I'm sorry. I'll be mean if she calls back."

"I'll want to poke her in the eye if she does."

Lucas chuckled and pulled her onto his lap. "I told her not to call back."

"No, you didn't. You said 'take care,'" she said, imitating his deep voice. "That's practically an invitation to visit— Ah," she sighed as he dipped his head and took her nipple in his mouth.

"Promise me you'll never do this with anyone else. Even if we break up. No more orgasms for any other woman," she managed to say, as his hand snaked up the leg of her gym shorts.

Lucas kissed her quiet, absorbing her tears, understanding her pain.

But she was leaving as soon as the weather broke, she'd told him. He'd be alone again.

He took her roughly, and made her scream this time. He wanted her to remember this coupling. But he wouldn't make a promise he couldn't keep.

The Goodfellows were fighting again and Doreen couldn't stand it. She and Lucas had left the confines of their bedroom to find the couple at war.

Lucas, on the other hand, seemed withdrawn. She knew he was itching to get out of the house, but the tremendous winds had discouraged him from venturing out, and he'd fallen into a sullen mood, walking the rooms of the house, checking for damage. Was it only the storm that put him in this funk? she wondered.

"Are you hungry?" she asked him.

"No." He looked at his watch for the tenth time. The lights flickered and the power died. "Brandon, let's check the garage for standing water."

The man hopped up, happy to get away from his wife. He put on a pair of waders Lucas brought him. They found brooms and went into the garage, chatting like old friends.

Doreen had expected Lucas to say something to her, but he didn't. His silence stung, but she refused to be wounded. "Mikaylah, let's make some sandwiches."

"Are you hungry again, Doreen? 'Cause, honey, if I eat any more, I might burst." She patted the tiny bump of a stomach and giggled.

"I don't really want to make sandwiches. I just need something to do. Plus, I think we're getting on the guys' nerves."

"I know I am." Mikaylah giggled and waved her hand. "Why don't we tackle that office? Have you seen it? Lucas obviously doesn't know a thing about filing, *or* billing, for that matter. Life is in the electronic age, but not Lucas."

"I've been here for days and haven't been to his office."

"Well, let me show you something new," Mikaylah said happily.

Doreen entered the biggest mess she'd seen in a

long time. There was paper covering every surface. It was like Lucas just walked in, set papers on flat surfaces and walked out, closing the door behind him.

Mikaylah put her hands on her hips. "Whatdoya-say? Candles and a bottle of wine?"

"I think I love you," Doreen said. They burst into giggles and hurried back toward the kitchen.

The storm rocked the house and they froze in place, then kept working. They started sorting and within the hour had gotten the papers into several workable piles.

Mikaylah organized receipts into folders while Doreen typed invoices. She knew she was using up Lucas's computer battery, but he had two nine-hour batteries, and she figured they'd use one today and another tomorrow if they had to.

They'd been at it for about three hours and had checked on the men twice but had been shooed away.

Lucas had built a strong house that was doing a good job of standing up to the hurricane's winds, so they stayed inside and worked, glad for the distraction.

"So what's the deal with you and Lucas?"

"We met through my former boss, and it's physical."

"Honey, I've been married longer than you've had your permanent teeth. You *love* that man."

Doreen stopped typing, the rain pounding the roof like boots. They stared at the roof until Mikaylah hit Doreen's shoulder.

"I do love him, Mikaylah. We've known each other for eight months and we've been together for two days, and he's all in me. I was crying earlier and I feel like crying now."

"That why he's so snappy? Because of all this love between you two?" She giggled like she'd won a prize. "I remember that feeling when I fell in love with Brandon. I'm forty-five now, honey, and I was twenty-two. Everybody thought I was crazy to fall in love with him. But he was handsome and he had a good job at the circus and great ideas. What wasn't to fall in love with? Honey, it took him years to turn into an asshole."

Doreen snickered. "Mikaylah," she chided.

"I know, I'm kidding. He wasn't always like the gruff man he is now. But he's changed. I divorced him last year."

"You did what?" Doreen stared at the tiny woman who made folders as she talked.

"I divorced him. He can be mean and demeaning, and I wasn't taking it anymore, so I left him. I went and got a town house and had a good time. I learned how to samba and tango and I took a vacation by myself. All the things he didn't want to do. But I missed him. Life out there wasn't better, so we decided to try to make it work."

"Is it working?"

"Yes," she nodded. "It might not look like it, but we love each other. Brandon's a good man. He's generous and kind, and he wants the world to see him as a tall, big man. He doesn't realize that I already see him that way."

A tearing sound started and they both looked up. "That doesn't sound good," Doreen said. She looked around the room with the help of her candle.

"There's a crack in the foundation," Mikaylah called out, as she pointed at an outside wall.

Doreen saw what Mikaylah was talking about, and without speaking the two women went into action.

"Help me!" she screamed.

They moved file cabinets to shore up the wall, but the crack grew wider.

Mikaylah ran to the kitchen and got the last roll of duct tape. They cut tape and applied tape to the wall until there wasn't any left, and still with every crack of thunder it seemed another inch grew in the wall.

When the wall shook, they looked at each other, grabbed the computers and Doreen screamed, "Run!"

Lucas was sure his eyes were playing tricks on him as he and Brandon stood in the shed waiting for the right time to run back over to the house. He saw a pink slicker and a seafoam-green slicker coming toward him, but they were somehow tethered. Then it hit him.

He smacked Brandon on the shoulder, and they took off running for the women.

His heart raced at the sight of Mikaylah taking flight and Doreen falling to the ground and pulling her back to earth by the rope.

Somehow their stupid plan was working. They were making their way to the shed.

"No!" he yelled, but his voice was snatched away by the wind.

Scared out of his mind, he ran into the wind, losing his footing. Brandon lassoed him and they got to the women at the same time. A loud roar made them turn around, just in time to see Ms. Lucy's roof ripped off her house.

Lucas reached out for Doreen, but he was too late. Flying debris whipped around, hit her in the head and knocked her to the ground. She lay there, unmoving.

Chapter 17

Fear galvanized Lucas, and he scrambled forward to pull the storm-tossed debris off Doreen, Nails and wood pricked and splintered his hands, but he paid them no mind as he gathered Doreen in his arms.

From a distance he heard Mikaylah scream. Turning in that direction, he saw Brandon pulling her toward the house.

He picked up Doreen and staggered to the house, tossed from side to side in the wind.

Prayers ran through his mind, scriptures his mother had taught him. He repeated them like a mantra as he forged through the hurricane.

He cursed himself for leaving her in the house. He should have been in there with her. He'd said he would take care of her. He'd told her to trust him.

They entered through the garage. Lucas manually pulled down the door and secured it with the latches he'd installed after the last storm. Brandon got the women inside, carrying Mikaylah to the closet first, then Doreen, who was at least a foot taller than he.

Lucas brought buckets of water from the tub, and while Brandon worked on Mikaylah—who had a nasty bump on the back of her head, a gash on her leg and scrapes and bruises everywhere—Lucas focused all his attention on pulling shards of glass from Doreen's hand.

Brandon had been a medic in the circus and knew how to care for wounds, so Lucas followed his direction. He cleaned her up as best he could, guilt and fear thickening his voice as he called her name.

"I'm fine," she told him when she could finally speak. "Office there's wall in a crack." Then she closed her eyes.

Brandon scrunched his nose up and came to look at Doreen. He ran his hands along her neck and skull. "She's got a concussion. She's just saying things a little backward. That will straighten itself out. Keep her awake. Is she allergic to anything?"

Lucas shrugged. "I don't know."

"Grapefruit," Mikaylah said weakly. "It makes her lips burn. No acidic fruit. Cantaloupe, melons. She loves pineapple, but she only eats…"

"Little a," Doreen said.

"A little," Mikaylah translated.

Not knowing those details acted like a microcosm for all the ways Lucas had failed her. His emotions threatened to get the better of him, but Brandon clapped him on the back. "You're doing fine. Just keep them talking. With a concussion you want to keep them still but awake."

Lucas thanked him. "I'm going to get them some dry clothes."

Doreen tried to stand, and Lucas settled her. "I need you to watch Mikaylah, Doreen. She's hurt bad. Can you make sure she stays lying down?" He knew putting her in charge of Mikaylah's care would be the only way Doreen would take care of herself.

True to form, she lay back down beside her friend.

Lucas tore up the closet looking for dry clothes, but there was so much stuff in there he couldn't find anything. "I don't have anything. Where are Mikaylah's dry clothes?"

"Red suitcase, but if you have sweatpants and a button-up top that would be better."

"I've got that right here," he said, relieved to finally be able to help. He was worried that Doreen seemed to have lost her ability to say things correctly. He wanted her to be better. He wanted whatever was wrong with her to go away.

Lucas held up a blanket while Brandon changed his wife's clothes and then took the bloody, wet clothes to the laundry room. He was wondering what would have brought the women out into the storm when he heard terrible banging in his office.

Opening the door, he saw the breached wall and his heart thundered. They'd been in here cleaning up, he could tell. All the paper was gone. The wall had cracked, but they'd piled all the furniture against it and duct taped the wall. They were amazing.

Lord have mercy.

He closed the door and went back to the closet and Doreen watched him, her eyes filling with tears. "Sorry, I'm. Sorry."

"Me, too, baby. It's my fault. I shouldn't have left you in here. I was stupid for leaving you two inside. Come on. Let's get these wet clothes off so you can get comfortable."

He took off her wet top and slipped on a dry Florida Marlins T-shirt. But her pants proved more difficult. Tight wet denim was like a second skin.

"You'll feel better," Lucas told her, and Doreen shook her head but he knew she meant yes. He unzipped her pants and finally got her into dry sweats. He tossed everything into his bathroom, then brought them all pain meds for their headaches and water.

Lucas and Brandon cleaned up the space as much as possible, making it as user-friendly as they could.

"We should settle in for the night," Brandon told him when they were done.

"Yeah, I don't think I'm going to do much sleeping. Since Doreen has a concussion, I've got to keep her awake."

"Lucas," Doreen called. "We can just lie down."

He grabbed the pillows from the bed, and gave Brandon one and kept one, then curled up with Doreen.

The closet was dark except for the one flashlight that Brandon stood up in the corner.

"Mind if we listen to Terrence for a while?" Brandon asked. "Mikaylah loves him."

"He's my best friend and Doreen loves him, too," Lucas told him.

He was glad to wrap Doreen in the blankets that had been brought in earlier. "How's your head, baby?"

"Hurts."

A loud crash and glass shattering broke the silence, causing them to jump, but Brandon quieted everyone, reassuring them that the house was strong and could withstand anything because his friend Lucas had built it.

Lucas soothed Doreen. "It's okay, baby. We're doing fine."

He finally lay down and curled around Doreen so they could sleep, her hair loose and wild the way he liked it. She turned in to him.

"I love you, Lucas," she said, tossing and turning, her breath catching when a noise scared her.

She'd jump and he'd hold her and try to quiet her.

"Tell her you love her," Brandon told him. "Lie on top of her. She can't hear you if you don't speak to her heart. Inside she's afraid."

Mikaylah hadn't made a sound in hours, but Brandon hadn't stopped talking to her.

In the dim glow of the flashlight, Lucas could see how troubled Doreen's features were, and his heart broke. He did love her.

"I love you, too, Doreen."

Her head jerked away from his chest. "Mama, help me."

Tears burned his eyes. "No, baby, I'm here." He kissed her eyes and her ears and she pushed him away.

He caught her hand and put it against his face. "It's me, Lucas."

She settled down and he held her until she was restful, but it was inevitable that another crash would shake the house and she would cry out again.

He lay on top of her and talked to her until she fell back asleep. "I love you, Doreen. I love you, baby." Her heartbeat settled and she held him and slept under him all night long.

The generator had kicked in hours ago and cool air settled them all. It was Mikaylah that roused them.

"Brandon, I feel like there's an elephant on my chest. I need to go to the hospital."

"I didn't need to be admitted to the hospital."

Doreen looked at the stuffed animals Lucas had brought her and wished she didn't feel so foolish. He'd been at her side since she'd been admitted three days ago, and now it was time to go home. The hospital didn't have enough wheelchairs to go around, so she'd promised to walk out of the hospital under escort of a nurse and Lucas.

"I wish you'd stop telling yourself that lie," Lucas said. "You had a blood clot."

"Well, it's gone now." She eased off the bed and reached to get her sweater at the end of the bed.

"Are you an acrobat now? I can get that for you." He seemed so strong, but he looked like he still felt guilty. For the past three days Lucas had done everything to show his love for her, but she knew. In her heart, she knew.

"You have to stop doing things for me," she told him, their faces almost touching. Her flight to New York was leaving in three hours.

"Why?" Lucas was standing so close, she couldn't smell anything but him.

"Because I'm about to go home."

Stephen and Terrence stuck their heads into her room. "Hey there," Stephen said. He'd been the first to get to them at the house, and he'd taken them to the hospital.

"Hi," Doreen said. She reached up to hug the men who'd showered her with love since she'd been admitted. "I'm so glad to see you. Where are the girls?" she asked affectionately of their gorgeous women. They'd come the previous night, and washed and conditioned her hair, playing beauty shop until the nurses shooed them away late in the evening. They'd become like her girlfriends from home.

"Mia is meeting with Mo at your house about the reconstruction, and Sherri is at the store restocking your pantry. They send their love," Terrence said.

Lucas and Doreen were shocked. "They don't have to do that," Lucas said.

"This is Sherri and Mia," Terrence told him. "I think you'd better let them do their thing and accept graciously." He patted Lucas on the back. "How you holding up?"

"It was only a couple stitches. Brandon and I did well. Our focus was on the girls. We feel terrible they got hurt."

Stephen smiled at Doreen. "She survived. Look at

her. She's pretty, and strong, and she's a hero. I heard from Brandon she saved Mikaylah from blowing away." He turned to Lucas and his smile disappeared. "I hear the wall in your office is one for the books, though."

Doreen rested her head on Lucas's shoulder. She loved all of them. This was what a family was all about. "We didn't want the wall to come down."

Lucas kissed her forehead. "I don't care about the wall as long as you're okay."

"They finally released me," Doreen told the men.

"So they're letting you fly home?" Terrence asked, looking disappointed.

"Yes, my flight is in three hours." Doreen's eyes watered and Lucas rubbed her back.

"We'd just gotten her to the place where she'd stopped crying. Thanks, T."

"You mean all my hard work of getting those nails in that tire were for nothing?" Terrence protested. "I nearly broke my back."

"I told you I couldn't participate in the commission of a felony," Stephen said. "I looked away," he added, grinning.

Doreen's mouth fell open, and she threw her arms around Terrence and then Stephen. "I love you both so much! You're my big brothers. Only brothers would do something so malicious out of love."

Everyone in the room burst out laughing as Doreen dabbed her teary eyes.

"You owe me two hundred dollars for that tire," Lucas told them, kidding.

"Yeah, the check's in the mail. I have news."

Terrence held up his hands. "Sherri and I are engaged."

"Terrence," Lucas said softly, "I'm really happy for you."

Doreen looked at Lucas and tried not to cry. Lucas didn't know that some of the words he'd whispered to her the night of the storm had gotten through to her. She'd heard him say he loved her. She'd felt him crying over her and praying to God and her mother to help her get better.

But she couldn't say anything. Those moments were private, between him and God and her mom. If he asked her, she'd commit her life to him, too.

"Congratulations," she said, hugging Terrence again. "I'll call Sherri when I get home. We'd better say goodbye to Brandon and Mikaylah and get to the airport."

She took Lucas's hand and walked out, plastering a brave but false smile on her face.

The island had taken a beating from the hurricane. Trees were down, and many houses were damaged while others were gone.

"Lucas, what happened to the house we stopped at when I first got here?"

"It didn't make it, baby."

"Did everyone make it out okay?"

He shook his head. "I don't know."

She unbuckled her seat belt and leaned over. Lucas did what he'd been doing for the past week. He put his arms around her.

Doreen turned her head so he wouldn't see her

crying. They were on the airport property heading toward the airline.

"You sure you don't want to stay?" he said.

"I want to," she said. "But you know I can't. This is the job I've been wanting forever. I just want to try it. I'll come back," she said, not able to hide her tears anymore. "I promise."

Doreen put her hand over her mouth to get hold of her emotions, and Lucas parked and pulled her bags from the back. She didn't want him to think she was like Emma. A woman that would make empty promises and not come back to him. She took his hand. "Believe me, I'll be back."

"I know."

"Don't fall in love with anyone else. Promise me."

"I promise."

Her breath caught and she leaned back and looked at him.

"You do?" Tears clouded her eyes.

"Yes, baby. I won't love another woman like I love you. I won't make another woman come like you. I won't touch another woman like I touch you. Ever. I love only you. Forever."

His tender kisses melted her heart and she wondered again why she was going back to New York. She didn't want to leave him. Everything about it felt wrong, but she still felt compelled to go, so she was following her one last instinct that said *go home.* She was going to board the plane and leave.

"Will you kiss me before I go inside? I don't want to kiss in the security line. I might start crying again."

"Like now?" he said, his smile wry.

Doreen wiped her eyes. She didn't want to leave him, but this was her big break.

"Will you visit me?"

"Yes, baby. Come on."

He carried the bags and Doreen walked alongside him up to the skycap.

"How many traveling today?"

"None," she said.

"Two," Lucas said at the same time.

"What did you say?" she asked him.

"Two. Both of us are going to New York."

"Why? I don't want to go, now. I want to stay here with you."

His lips closed over hers and he lifted her off her feet. She used to hate being picked up, but she was in love and she just didn't care anymore.

"Excuse me, we have a flight to catch," a woman said from behind them.

Lucas carried her out of the way and let the people go around them.

Doreen looked at the man she loved and saw the love in his eyes. "My heart is beating so fast," she whispered, and hugged him. "Why are you coming?" she asked.

"Because you can't stop crying."

She put her arms around him. "I'm going to stop. Look, I know you have work to do. I know you have to put the house back together again."

He chuckled and handed their tickets to the skycap along with their luggage.

"Lucas, why are you coming to New York?"

"Because I wasn't being fair to make you choose between me and your job. I wanted that house so badly and it was almost destroyed. But if I'd lost you, my world would have ended."

He held her and she knew they'd be together forever. He'd been there when she'd been so afraid she could have chosen death over life.

There had been moments when she'd awakened to find his hands on her body as he prayed for her, or his hands joined in prayer with Brandon as they prayed for all of them. She'd known then.

He accepted their tickets from the skycap and tipped him. Then he guided her to the side. "I can't lose you. Distance and time mean something to me now. They mean everything to me now, Doreen. You mean everything to me. That's why I'm coming to New York."

She put her head on his chest. "What about the house?" she asked.

"Mo will start working on it tomorrow, and when we come back it'll be in better shape than it is now."

"When are we coming back?"

"When you're ready."

She couldn't have loved him more. "Six weeks," she said.

"Then six weeks. You promised Horatio an internship and we should see that through, right?"

Doreen nodded through her tears as she kissed his lips. "Yes, we should."

"And I want to meet all your friends and let them work me over. Ask the hard questions and make sure I'm right for you."

"I know you're right for me."

"I also want you to do your job."

"Lucas, I don't want that job anymore. I know what I'm walking away from. My job now will be finding my replacement. Sherri told me about a job down here that sounds perfect for me."

"Baby, that's really good, but once, a long time ago, I asked a woman to give up a job for me, and she didn't. Luckily, I found the right woman from the wrong situation." Lucas took her hand and they walked into the airport and got in the line for security. "The woman I love is in the same predicament as I was, and I don't want her finding a man to replace me. She lives out of state."

She smiled up at him and bit his chin, and he burst out laughing. "But this time I'm smarter. I want my lady to know that I'm there for her as much as she's there for me."

"I love you down in here." She pointed to her chest.

He caressed her cheek. "Take this chance to make everything right with your job and your friends. They've been there through it all, so it's only fair."

Love radiated from his eyes and bathed her in warmth. "What will you do for six weeks?" she asked him.

"I'm an architect, baby. I've got plenty of work to do. There are brownstones everywhere for sale. Your building, too," he told her.

"How do you know that?"

"This is what I do." He kissed her nose, sending a thrill through her body. "Who knows? We might stay a while."

Doreen threw her arms around his neck and rocked

him. "I love you for even thinking about it, but if you think I'm staying longer than six weeks, you can forget it."

His eyes softened and changed, and she knew he would give her the world. "Doreen Elizabeth Gamble, I love you, too."

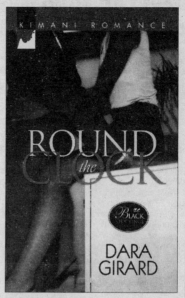

REQUEST YOUR FREE BOOKS!

2 FREE NOVELS
PLUS 2 FREE GIFTS!

KIMANI™ ROMANCE

Love's ultimate destination!

YES! Please send me 2 FREE Kimani™ Romance novels and my 2 FREE gifts (gifts are worth about $10). After receiving them, if I don't wish to receive any more books, I can return the shipping statement marked "cancel." If I don't cancel, I will receive 4 brand-new novels every month and be billed just $4.69 per book in the U.S. or $5.24 per book in Canada. That's a savings of over 20% off the cover price. It's quite a bargain! Shipping and handling is just 50¢ per book.* I understand that accepting the 2 free books and gifts places me under no obligation to buy anything. I can always return a shipment and cancel at any time. Even if I never buy another book from Kimani Press, the two free books and gifts are mine to keep forever.

168 XDN EYQG   368 XDN EYQS

Name	(PLEASE PRINT)
Address	Apt. #
City	State/Prov. Zip/Postal Code

Signature (if under 18, a parent or guardian must sign)

Mail to **The Reader Service:**
IN U.S.A.: P.O. Box 1867, Buffalo, NY 14240-1867
IN CANADA: P.O. Box 609, Fort Erie, Ontario L2A 5X3

Not valid to current subscribers of Kimani Romance books.

**Want to try two free books from another line?
Call 1-800-873-8635 or visit www.morefreebooks.com.**

* Terms and prices subject to change without notice. Prices do not include applicable taxes. Sales tax applicable in N.Y. Canadian residents will be charged applicable provincial taxes and GST. Offer not valid in Quebec. This offer is limited to one order per household. All orders subject to approval. Credit or debit balances in a customer's account(s) may be offset by any other outstanding balance owed by or to the customer. Please allow 4 to 6 weeks for delivery. Offer available while quantities last.

KROM09

HELP CELEBRATE
ARABESQUE'S
15TH ANNIVERSARY!

ARABESQUE®

2009 marks Arabesque's 15th anniversary!

Help us celebrate by telling us about your most special memories and moments with Arabesque books. Entries will be judged by the Arabesque Anniversary Committee based on which are the most touching and well written. Fifteen lucky winners will receive as a prize a full-grain leather duffel bag with the Arabesque anniversary logo.

How to Enter: To enter, hand-print (or type) on an 8 ½" x 11" plain piece of paper your full name, mailing address, telephone number and a description of your most special memories and moments with Arabesque books (in two hundred [200] words or less) and send it to "Arabesque 15th Anniversary Contest 20901"—in the U.S.: Kimani Press, 233 Broadway, Suite 1001, New York, NY 10279, or in Canada: 225 Duncan Mill Road, Don Mills, ON M3B 3K9. No other method of entry will be accepted. The contest begins on July 1, 2009, and ends on December 31, 2009. Entries must be postmarked by December 31, 2009, and received by January 8, 2010. A copy of these Official Rules is available online at www.myspace.com/kimanipress, or to obtain a copy of these Official Rules (prior to November 30, 2009), send a self-addressed, stamped envelope (postage not required from residents of VT) to "Arabesque 15th Anniversary Contest 20901 Rules," 225 Duncan Mill Road, Don Mills, ON M3B 3K9. Limit one (1) entry per person. If more than one (1) entry is received from the same person, only the first eligible entry submitted will be considered. By entering the contest, entrants agree to be bound by these Official Rules and the decisions of Harlequin Enterprises Limited (the "Sponsor"), which are final and binding.

NO PURCHASE NECESSARY. Open to legal residents of U.S. and Canada (except Quebec) who have reached the age of majority at time of entry. Void where prohibited by law. Approximate retail value of each prize: $131.00 (USD).

VISIT **WWW.MYSPACE.COM/KIMANIPRESS**
FOR THE COMPLETE OFFICIAL RULES

KPI5ARACONTEST